Tl House

by

Kathi Daley

This book is a work of fiction. Names, characters, places, and incidents either are products of the author's imagination or are used fictitiously. Any resemblance to actual events or locales or persons, living or dead, is entirely coincidental.

Copyright © 2018 by Katherine Daley

Version 1.0

Chapter 1

Friday, October 19

Every town has one. A big old house that has stood empty for so long, no one remembers anyone living there. The iconic subject of lore and folktales that hints at supernatural occurrences, tragedy, and family curses that can be neither confirmed nor denied. For the town of White Eagle, Montana, the house that serves as the subject of ghostly stories by the campfire is a huge old mansion built more than sixty years ago by a wealthy industrialist as a country home for his wife and five children. The house, devoid of love and laughter, served as a sort of luxury prison far away from the hustle and bustle of Hartford Harrington's full and busy life in San Francisco.

Structurally, Harrington House had weathered the long winters and hot summers of northern Montana. It had endured long after all but one of those five children had been buried in the little family cemetery at the edge of the huge estate. I'm not sure why the place was never sold, or even lived in, by whichever Harrington relation inherited the property, but after the summer Houston Harrington jumped from the third-floor window to the concrete bricks of the veranda below, not a single Harrington or heir had set foot in the place.

"Morning, Tess, Tilly," greeted Hap Hollister, as my golden retriever and I entered his home and hardware store to deliver the daily mail, along with a generous dollop of local news.

"I love the Halloween decorations you put in the window. The cobwebs and spiders are very believable," I jumped right in after setting the stack of mail I'd brought on the counter.

"I hope not too believable." Hap chuckled. "I wouldn't want to scare away potential customers."

"Combined with the big orange pumpkins and jolly scarecrow, I think the window is just right. It's very inviting."

Hap picked up the mail I had set on the counter and began thumbing through it. "Glad to hear it. I noticed your mom did her window up right nice too."

"As you're aware, the Halloween town Mom and Aunt Ruthie display is a White Eagle tradition. It does seem the train Aunt Ruthie sent away for added a nice element this year."

"And that new haunted mansion she set off to the side. I love that the lights inside flash and there's a crackling sound every now and then that provides a very spooky feel."

"I guess every Halloween town needs a spooky Halloween house." I leaned a hip against the counter as Tilly sat patiently at my feet. "Speaking of spooky Halloween houses, did you hear someone moved into the Harrington place?"

"You don't say. About time someone brought some life to it. She's much too grand a lady to sit empty and unloved for so long."

I rested my elbows on the counter and leaned in. "Maybe, but everyone says it's haunted. I'm not sure why anyone would buy a haunted old house in the middle of nowhere."

Hap's blue eyes, faded with age, sparkled as he leaned his head of white hair in closer to my brown mane. "Guess there are some folks who either don't believe in ghosts, or aren't scared of them if they do. Personally, I like to think I rank among the latter."

My head tilted with curiosity. "So you believe in ghosts?"

Hap nodded. "Have to. Seen a few. Do you know anything about the new owner?"

"His name is Jordan Westlake. He's thirty-two, single, and, from what I hear, quite the babe."

"Babe?"

"He's handsome. In a cute and charming sort of way. I hear he's loaded and has plans to completely renovate the house from top to bottom."

Hap's eyes grew two sizes. "You don't say. Seems as the only home and hardware store in town, I might want to introduce myself to him. I'm sure Mr. Westlake is going to be needing supplies. Paint and such."

I grinned. "I'm sure he will. Bree told me Westlake is related to the San Francisco Westlakes, and one of the heirs to Walter Westlake's fortune." Bree Price was a bookstore owner and my best friend and had taken the time to look him up. Walter Westlake had built an import empire several generations back. "I figured if he's that rich he'll just hire a contractor, but Bree said she read a newspaper article that said he plans to do a lot of the work on the house himself, only hiring out the plumbing, electrical, and heavy hauling. From what Bree was able to sleuth out, it looks like Jordan Westlake is, and always has been, rich enough so he never needed to work, so he took up a hobby: restoring old things and giving them new life."

"I'm anxious to meet this young man. He sounds like the sort I'd get along with just fine. Coffee?" Hap nodded toward the pot on his counter.

"Thanks, but I really should run. I'm supposed to hang out with Tony tonight and I don't want to be late."

"If you're going to see Tony, tell him that paint he ordered for his own remodel is in. I was going to call him, but the boy never seems to answer his dang blasted phone."

I laughed. "You know how it is when there's a genius at work. The rest of the world sort of fades away. I'll let him know about the paint."

After I left Hap's, I headed across the street to the White Eagle Police Station. My brother, Mike Thomas, should be in his office at this time of day, which meant I could firm up plans for tomorrow while delivering his mail. Mike, Bree, Tony, and I planned to have dinner together at a new restaurant that had just opened up down by the lake. I also wanted to speak to his partner, Frank Hudson. I wondered if he had any information regarding White

Eagle's newest resident. Frank, you see, in addition to being an all-around nice guy, excellent cop, and Mike's best friend, was a bit of a gossip. I was pretty sure if there was news, he'd be the one to ask about it.

"Morning, Frank," I greeted as I dropped his mail on his desk.

"Morning, Tess, Tilly."

"Any news on the newest member of our community?"

Frank leaned forward and lowered his voice, although we were the only two in the room. "I heard Jordan Westlake arrived in town yesterday afternoon, and according to Toby Tanner, who we know is a bit of a snoop, he spent the whole night holed up inside that huge, dusty old house."

"Really?" I had to admit I was surprised. I guess I just imagined a rich man would stay in a hotel while the place was being renovated. "Was the electricity and water even on?"

"Water and gas were turned on yesterday. Electricity will be on today. Toby said Westlake showed up with a fancy SUV filled with all sorts of camping equipment. It looks as if he plans to set up a tent in the middle of his living room."

I couldn't help but frown. "How exactly does Toby know all this?"

"Toby's been camping in the woods just behind the house. He brought his binoculars and enough food to last a week. He said he wanted to be in a position to see everything that went on from the very beginning."

"Does Mr. Westlake know he has a man with binoculars squatting on his property?"

Frank shrugged. "He hasn't lodged a complaint. If he does, I guess I'll have to run Toby off. In the meantime, I admit to being curious to find out what, if anything, he's able to see. He even brought a video recorder, which he promised to use only if a ghost shows up."

"Does Mike know about all this?" My brother was a bit more of a stickler for the rules than Frank, and I could see how he might object to Toby basically stalking Westlake.

"Haven't talked to him about it, but I haven't kept it from him either. Guess he might have heard something along the way. What he knows and what he doesn't know isn't a concern of mine."

I lifted a brow. "I sort of think Mike's going to see things differently. You should tell him what you know before he finds out from someone else."

"Someone else like you?" Frank said with a tone of accusation in his voice.

I held up my hands in my own defense. "I'm not saying a word. I am saying, though, that someone other than me might decide to tell Mike what's going on out at the old mansion."

Frank made a face. "I suppose I might mention it to him if it comes up in conversation."

I picked up my mailbag and prepared to head down the hallway to Mike's office. "Did Toby happen to mention what he observed last night?"

"Lights. Like from a candle or a flashlight, wandering from one room to the next for hours."

I shifted my bag onto my shoulder. "I guess Jordan Westlake might have been taking a look at his new place. Seems crazy to do it in the dark, though."

Frank winked. "Didn't say it was him causing the light to move around the house."

"You think someone else is there?"

"Some*one* or some*thing*."

I wasn't sure if I believed in ghosts, but I was pretty sure that if there were one or more living in the Harrington mansion, they wouldn't need a flashlight to see to get around. I was willing to bet Frank knew that as well. If I had to guess, he was just trying to scare me, but Tess Thomas didn't scare easily.

"Morning, Mike," I said after tapping three times on his open door.

He looked up from the report he was reading. "Morning, Tess, Tilly."

I set Mike's mail on his desk, then sat down on the chair across the desk from him. "Heard Jordan Westlake arrived yesterday."

"Yeah, I heard too."

"I'm kind of interested to meet him. From what Bree said, he's handsome and rich, but he must also be unique to have bought such a rundown old house with plans to renovate it with his own hands."

"Bree said he was handsome and rich?"

I lifted a shoulder. "Everyone is saying it."

Mike sighed.

"Can you blame them?" I added. "Having someone buy that old place and actually move into it after all these years is the most interesting thing to happen in White Eagle for quite some time."

"He didn't buy it," Mike said.

I tilted my head. "He didn't buy it?"

"He inherited it. His mother was a Harrington before she married a Westlake. She was the closest heir, and she left the house to her youngest son, Jordan."

"I thought none of the five Harrington offspring married or had children. That's the story I've heard my whole life anyway. It seemed every one of those five children died before reaching adulthood. Houston Harrington, the youngest and last survivor, was just fourteen when he jumped from the third-floor window and killed himself shortly after his twin sister died."

"As far as I know that's true, but it seems Francine Westlake was adopted by Hartford Harrington when he married his second wife, Anastasia Pembroke, who had a daughter from a previous relationship."

"Wait." I held up a hand. "What happened to Hartford's first wife? The mother of the five children?"

"She died, most say of a broken heart, shortly after moving into the house."

Wow. This really was a depressing story. I wasn't sure I wanted to hear the rest, but I did want to hear about Jordan Westlake. "Okay, so Francine Harrington became Hartford Harrington's heir and married a Westlake."

"Donovan Westlake. Donovan Westlake and Francine Harrington had four sons. Jordan is the youngest. Francine Harrington Westlake recently passed, and in her will she left Harrington House to Jordan. I guess he isn't overly bothered by the fact that six people all related to him by adoption died while living in that house more than fifty years ago."

"Given the fact that he's here now, I guess not."

I stood up and slipped my bag back onto my shoulder. As interesting as this conversation was, I needed to get a move on if I was going to finish my route in time to go home and change before heading out to Tony's. "Are we still planning to meet at Bree's tomorrow night?"

"Short of an emergency, I'll be there."

I motioned to Tilly, then headed back down the hallway. Mike and Bree had settled into a committed relationship over the past few months. At first, I'll admit it felt odd that my brother and my best friend had feelings for each other, but after watching them together and realizing I'd never seen either of them happier, I found myself pulling for them to make it as a couple. Of course, it also made me nervous, and my nervousness made me spend quite a lot of time wondering if it was wise for friends to become intimate. Tony had told me that, in his opinion, friendship could be the basis for the most powerful love two people can have. His words rang true, but I worried that if Mike and Bree's relationship didn't stand the test of time, the comfortable companionship we'd all had since childhood would never be the same.

I thought back to my own almost pivotal moment with Tony, who, other than Bree, was my very best friend. I wasn't sure where the moment had come from, but on the same day Mike and Bree got together last spring, Tony and I found ourselves on the verge of bringing our own sexual tension to its logical conclusion. I've thought about it at least a million times since, and wondered what would have happened if Tony's dog, Titan, hadn't lumbered over and ruined the moment. Part of me was disappointed the kiss hadn't happened, but mostly, I was glad we hadn't taken a step that might lead to the end of the friendship we'd always had.

Bree thought I was crazy for not following through with my intensifying feelings for Tony, but I'd seen friendships ruined after sex was introduced into the relationship. Inevitably, the passion of new intimacy faded, and then all that remained of what was once a strong bond were hurt feelings that could never be overcome. No, I'd decided on numerous occasions, my feelings for Tony were too important to gamble on.

"Morning, Mom, Aunt Ruthie," I said as I walked into their diner, with Tilly tagging along behind me. It really did look festive. In addition to the Halloween village and model train in the window, Mom had strung up orange lights that were wrapped in colorful fall garlands.

"Is there mail from overseas?" Mom started hopefully.

I shook my head. "Sorry." My mom had been hoping for a card or letter from her own complicated love interest, Romero Montenegro. He lived and worked in Italy, but he and Mom had participated in a brief long-distance relationship that, based on the lack of correspondence in more than two months, seemed to have fizzled out.

"I should have taken the time off and gone to Italy when he asked." Mom groaned.

I wanted to remind her that her fling with Romero had been ill-advised from the beginning, but instead I held my tongue and gave her a hug. "I'm sorry, Mom. I know you enjoyed your friendship with him."

Mom let out a breath. "I suppose it's for the best. It's not like we ever had a future. I live here in Montana and he lives across the ocean." Mom gave a sad little smile. "It was fun while it lasted."

I didn't want her to be sad, but I also didn't want to think about my middle-aged mother having *fun* with a single playboy more than a decade younger, so I changed the subject. "Did you hear Jordan Westlake is in town?"

"I heard he arrived yesterday," Aunt Ruthie trilled. "People have been talking about it all day."

"I still don't quite understand what he plans to do with that huge old house," Mom said. "It doesn't seem like a practical choice for a single man."

"According to Mike, he didn't choose it. It chose him."

Mom frowned, confused.

"He inherited it," I clarified.

"Inherited it? I wonder if he means to keep it."

I shrugged. "The thing interests me more than I feel it ought to. Everyone says the place is haunted, and I've heard the story about the tragedy that met the family for whom the house was built. I'm not sure I'd set foot in it if that had happened to mine."

"I seem to remember Hartford Harrington moved his wife and children into the place but then went back to his life in the city," Aunt Ruthie said.

Mom nodded. "It's true. And they stayed even after the daughter went missing just months after they arrived."

"Missing?" I asked. "I'd heard all the children died. I didn't know one went missing. What happened?"

"The oldest daughter, Hillary Harrington, was just fourteen when they moved into the big house in the woods. I'm not sure why they moved to White Eagle from San Francisco in the first place, but I do remember reading that after Hartford Harrington went back to the city, strange things began happening. The locals believed the family had brought some sort of curse with them from San Francisco. I don't know if that's true, but two months after they came to town, Hillary Harrington went missing. Her bloody clothes were found in the woods behind the house. It was assumed she'd met with foul play, but her body was never found and her killer, if there was one, was never identified."

I put a hand to my mouth. "That's awful. The poor girl. Her poor mother."

Mom ran a rag over the counter of the currently empty café. "I can't imagine losing a child and never knowing what happened to her. It has to be more heartbreaking than is bearable. But she not only lost a daughter. Her oldest son died just a few weeks later."

I gasped. "How?"

"He was shot."

My eyes grew large. "Who shot him?"

"A man named Wilbur Woodbine. It seems Hudson Harrington believed it was Wilbur who'd killed his sister and hid her body, so even though he was only sixteen and Wilbur was a grown man, he went to confront him. Hudson had a gun, but so did Wilbur. In the end, it was Hudson who lost his life."

"And Wilbur?" I asked. "What happened to him?"

Mom shook her head. "Nothing. There was never any proof he'd killed Hillary, and it was decided the shooting was in self-defense."

I glanced at the clock. I wanted to hear the rest of the story, but I had my route to finish. "How do you know all this?" I asked as I hitched my bag onto my shoulder.

"I did a report on the family when I was in high school. I can fill you in on the rest sometime, but I can see you need to get back to work, so I won't keep you."

I took a step toward the door. "I'll come by tomorrow."

Chapter 2

I'm not sure how I pulled it off, but somehow, I managed to finish my route and then get back to my cabin in time to change before I needed to leave for Tony's. The days had grown short and a hint of winter was in the air, so I wore black jeans with black knee-high boots and a fuzzy gold sweater with hints of orange. Yes, I'll admit I did look somewhat like a pumpkin, but it was October, and with Halloween just around the corner, I was feeling festive and wanted to show it. In fact, I thought to myself as I grabbed a jacket from the closet, I might even stop by Hap's tomorrow to pick up some orange lights and pumpkin-scented candles for my little cabin in the woods.

As for tonight, Tony and I planned to have dinner and then play a new video game he'd been asked to preview. It seemed he had new games almost every time we got together. Of course, he'd made a name for himself in the gaming community, and developers valued the input he was happy to provide.

Tony had suggested I stay over, which was a good idea because our video nights usually went long. So, in addition to grabbing food, bedding, and toys for Tilly, as well as my cats, Tang and Tinder, I packed an overnight bag for myself. It was more and more common for me to stay at Tony's when I planned to hang out with him on the weekend. Bree was totally focused on spending every spare moment with Mike, so it was Tony who helped me fill my free time. At least when he wasn't working and had a bit of free time himself, which, given the huge project he'd been contracted to complete for NSA—the National Security Agency—hadn't been all that often.

I'd agreed to run an adoption clinic at the local animal shelter on Saturday morning because shelter owner and town veterinarian Brady Baker had rescue training with his dog Tracker. Brady and Tracker had joined the local search-and-rescue squad, and they took training and rescue simulations seriously. Brady's assistant, Lilly, would be around to handle things at the veterinary clinic, so all I needed to do was organize the other volunteers, then handle the adoption paperwork and screening. I figured I'd go back to Tony's afterward, so I packed clothes to wear to the clinic, which for this event required a costume, as well as casual clothing and something nicer to wear out to dinner with Bree and Mike.

I loaded the kids into the Jeep and headed up the mountain to Tony's. He lived on a private lake about twenty miles north of White Eagle. The drive up the narrow road that zigzagged up the mountain could be treacherous in the winter, but we'd only had light snow so far this season, which had melted soon after it fell. I turned on the radio just in time to catch an ad for the upcoming harvest festival. I hoped Tony would go with me next weekend because I was sure Bree would be going with Mike. The festival had been around since before I was born, and it was one of my favorite seasonal events. Not only was there an awesome haunted house, but there was pumpkin carving, hay rides, a street dance, and games and goodies for the kids too.

As soon as I arrived, Tony appeared at the front door, which was flanked by giant orange pumpkins. He waved and then came over to grab the things I'd brought for the animals, while I took out my overnight bag and the cat carrier holding Tang and Tinder. Tilly hopped out of the Jeep on her own and trotted over to greet Tony's dog, Titan, the minute he joined Tony. Titan and Tilly seemed to be in love. When together, they spent most of their time curled up in front of the fire.

"Your house looks awesome. I love the pumpkins on the porch and the little orange and white twinkle lights you strung in the trees."

"I took some time to decorate this afternoon. I knew you were coming and figured you'd appreciate the effort. I was going to put out the life-size monsters I bought last year, but I didn't have time. Maybe we can get to them this weekend."

"That would be fun. I enjoyed the way Herman and Boris would reach out as if they were going to grab me whenever I walked by. By the way, while we're on the subject of Halloween, do you want to go to the harvest festival together next weekend?"

"I'd like that." Tony smiled as we entered the house and he took my bag and set it aside. "I always look forward to the haunted house. I hear they hired a new company this year, so the props should be totally different from what we've seen in the past."

"I heard that too. In fact, I heard the company they hired this time is the one that did the big event in Saint Paul last year. I'm not sure why they agreed to come to tiny White Eagle, but unless my intel is wrong, we're in for something really special."

"It seems the company expanded, so they can do more than one town at a time," Tony confirmed.

"Speaking of haunted houses, did you know someone moved into the Harrington place?"

Tony looked surprised. "No, I didn't. I haven't been in town much lately. Did someone buy it?"

"Inherited." I went on to explain what I'd heard about the man who'd taken the plunge and planned to bring life to the place after more than fifty years.

Tony began to arrange pet beds and toys. "I'll have to look into the history of the house when I have a chance. It sounds interesting."

"The house and the family might have an interesting if tragic past. Digging into it might take some time. Did you finish that big project you've been working on?" I half-suspected he'd kept himself so engrossed in it as an excuse for us not to spend time together after the awkwardness of our almost-kiss on Mother's Day.

"I did, and it turned out well. I enjoy my work, but this project was especially intense and demanding. I think I'm going to take a break until after the holidays. I'd really like for us to spend more time together than we've been able to."

I couldn't quite keep my heart from going pitter-patter despite my best intentions. "I brought clothes and accessories to cover the whole weekend. I have the adoption clinic tomorrow morning, and then we have dinner with Mike and Bree at night, but maybe we can do some gaming tonight and on Sunday."

Tony squeezed my hand. "I'd planned to finish the decorating and work on my remodel, but I can do that while you're at the adoption clinic."

"Oh, about the remodel," I said before I forgot, "Hap said to tell you your paint is in."

"Perfect timing."

"I'll be in town anyway. I'll pick it up for you."

Tony smiled. "Thanks. That would be helpful."

"Are you still working on the kitchen?" Tony didn't cook often, but he liked to do it, so he'd decided on a complete remodel of what I'd considered an already exceptional kitchen.

"I'm just about done with it. I need to figure out what I'm going to do with the wall art I had before, but the room is completely functional. I'm planning to move on to the guest rooms this weekend. I was going to do the master bedroom first, but I still haven't made up my mind about a few things." Tony took my hand in his. "Come on. I'll show you what I've done in the kitchen."

I followed him across the large living area to the open cooking area. "I don't know why you're going to all this trouble. Your house is already magnificent."

Tony shrugged. "I guess I was in the mood for a change."

And what a change it was. "Wow." I was totally in love with the new kitchen. "I could probably live in this room."

"I thought it came out well. It has a warm, cozy feeling, but the appliances are restaurant grade. I'm glad you were able to come over tonight for the inaugural meal."

I sat down on a padded window seat that angled from the brick fireplace and looked out at the lake. "Something smells wonderful. What are we having?"

"Spinach-and-cheese-stuffed tortellini with a creamy saffron sauce."

"It not only smells like heaven but I'm starving. It's been a long day at the end of a long week."

Tony poured two glasses of wine and handed me one. "I just need to toss together the salad and heat the bread. If you want, you can have a seat at the counter and talk to me while I work."

"I love this window seat, but it can wait." I got up and crossed the room before sliding onto one of the stools Tony had bought to match the cabinets he'd installed to complement the new wood floor. I'd been working some on my own remodel, but I didn't have the eye, instinct, or budget Tony did, so my transformation wasn't going to be quite as grand. At least not yet.

"So, tell me what you know about the new owner of Harrington House," Tony requested as he began washing and chopping veggies for the salad.

"I don't know a lot. Jordan Westlake is a Harrington on his mother's side. He's also a San Francisco Westlake, which means he's loaded. Mike said he's already moved into the house and plans to do a lot of the work on it himself. Personally, if I had his kind of cash, I might just stay in a hotel until the remodel was complete, but he's supposed to be a hands-on guy."

"Sounds like someone I might enjoy getting to know. I have to assume he knows the house's history and has heard the rumors about it being haunted, so he must not be superstitious. If I remember correctly, Hartford Harrington's entire family died while living in that house."

"That's what I heard as well, though I don't know all the details. Mom said the oldest daughter, Hillary, was just fourteen when they moved into the house. She went missing, and her bloody clothes were found in the woods behind the house, but not her body. It was assumed she met with foul play, though her killer, assuming there was one, was never identified. A brother, Hudson, who was sixteen at the time, believed she was killed by a man named Wilbur Woodbine. Hudson confronted Woodbine and was shot and killed in the ensuing struggle."

Tony shook his head. "That's really sad."

"Woodbine insisted he was innocent of killing Hillary and charges were never brought against him for either death."

"It'd be interesting to do some digging into the history of the entire Harrington family. Do you know how the others died?"

I shook my head. "I'm not sure. Mom seemed to know, but I needed to finish my route, so I didn't have time for her to go over the whole family history. It's probably available online. Hartford Harrington was a rich, powerful, influential man. I'm sure there were all sorts of newspaper articles at the time."

"Maybe we can spend some time looking into it after we eat," Tony suggested.

I took a sip of my wine. "Have you been looking for news about my father?"

"I have an update, but let's eat first."

Great. Now I was going to be curious the entire time we spent on the meal, but a discussion revolving around the man who'd abandoned me and my family fifteen years ago probably wasn't appropriate dinner conversation. Just the thought of my father and the double life it seemed he'd been living was enough to give me indigestion.

As expected, the food was delicious. I offered to take the dogs out while Tony cleaned up the kitchen afterward. My mind had stayed focused almost exclusively on my father since Tony had mentioned he had an update. The situation was complex, so I knew I shouldn't expect much, but my mind would never be totally at rest until I was able to know for certain whether my father was dead or alive, and if he was alive, I needed to understand what he'd done and why he'd done it.

My search for my dad began when I was fifteen and nosing around in the attic of the house Mom, Mike, and I lived in. I found a letter hidden in a book I believed to be encrypted. The book had been stored with some things my dad had stored in the attic before he died in a fiery accident while driving the cross-country truck route he'd been working most of my life. Believing it could somehow provide an answer to the questions I'd had since his death, I wanted to try to break the code. After dozens of failed attempts, I enlisted Tony's help. As it turned out, the letter hadn't been encrypted at all, but our search had led us to uncover some anomalies in my father's death, what I'd suspected all along.

It took Tony twelve years to find the first clue, a photograph of a man who looked an awful lot like my dad standing in front of a building that was built less than ten years before. Because my dad was supposed to have died three years before that, I knew if the man in the photo was the man who'd given me piggyback rides and taken me camping, he couldn't have died when we were told he had.

A few months after finding that photo, Tony happened across one of a man in a convenience store just outside Gallup, New Mexico. The really odd thing was that Tony, even with all his techy know-how, couldn't figure out who'd taken it or posted it online. It wasn't part of the surveillance system in the minimart, and when Tony tried to trace the source, it came back as unknown, which concerned him. It was his belief that the photo had originated from someone who possessed a high level of security. Someone in the CIA, the NSA, or some other spy organization. Tony wanted to proceed with caution, especially after I received a call warning me to leave well enough alone.

I didn't want to think about my dad being a fugitive or a foreign spy, but the more we found out, the more it looked as if he might not be one of the good guys. Tony had tried to warn me about that possibility from the beginning. There were times I considered dropping the whole thing and getting on with my life, but in the end, I knew that wouldn't be possible until I knew one way or the other.

By the time Titan, Tilly, and I returned to the house, Tony had completed the kitchen cleanup. We got all four animals settled with toys in front of the television before going down to the basement, where Tony had built his clean room. It contained millions of dollars' worth of high-tech equipment, so in addition to being free of dust, it was secure.

"What did you find?" I asked in an effort to get the ball rolling the minute he sat down at one of the many terminals strategically placed around the room.

"Have a seat." Tony pulled up a chair next to him.

"Remember the photo we found last February, of the man with a beard standing on a bridge in Norway?"

"The one we matched with the passport photo of the man named Jared Collins, dated 1981?"

"Exactly."

"I remember. He looked as if he could have been my father when he was younger, but we didn't have any conclusive evidence of it. You were going to look for additional photos of Jared Collins, as well as additional photos of a young Grant Thomas."

"Which I did. If you remember, I found out the photo of the man we believe was Jared Collins was part of a surveillance report conducted by a private investigator working for Galvin Kline, a state senator."

"You said you were going to look for more photos as well as an explanation for why Kline was following Collins. Did you find something?"

Tony entered some commands into his computer program. "Not about Jared Collins. Not yet. I did find out, however, that Grant Walton Thomas didn't seem to exist prior to 1981."

I frowned. "What do you mean, he didn't exist?"

"I mean your father, Grant Walton Thomas, who, as far as you knew, was born on April 12, 1957, in Saint Louis, Missouri, doesn't have a paper trail of any sort until shortly before he married your mother. There are no school, work, financial records, nothing. If Grant Walton Thomas existed prior to 1981, it wasn't in this country. At least not under the name Grant Walton Thomas."

I put a hand to my racing heart. "So my father either lived in another country before 1981 or he lived in this country under a different name."

"That's what I suspect. If he came to the US from another country, I doubt he did so legally. I couldn't find evidence of a passport, visa, or anything else under the name Grant Walton Thomas. And there's more: If Grant Walton Thomas is still alive, which I suspect he might be, he's no longer using that name. Officially and legally, Grant Walton Thomas died in the truck accident. Whoever is walking around with your father's face is someone else now."

I put my hands on my head, as if to keep it from exploding. This was so surreal. "How? How does someone just disappear and then reappear as someone else? Don't you need things, proof, that you are who you say you are? How could he get a job or a driver's license or even a bank account without proof? How could he have obtained a marriage license?"

"There are ways to get fake IDs. Good ones. And I'm not just talking about a piece of paper but an entire history."

"If he had a fake history, wouldn't you have found it?"

Tony shrugged. "Maybe. Until we know more about what's going on, it will be hard to pinpoint what information might be real and what's been fabricated."

"What's the oldest paperwork you can find under the name Grant Walton Thomas?"

"A Montana state driver's license issued to a man using that name on May 17, 1981. He must have shown a birth certificate to obtain that, but I'm assuming it was fake. Currently, a certified birth certificate must be presented to obtain a driver's license, but back then, a legitimate-looking document was all that was needed. Grant Walton Thomas owned his own eighteen-wheeler. I found a tax return filed in that name in 1982. He was living in Bozeman when he married your mother that year. Mike was born in 1983, and shortly after, your parents and brother moved to White Eagle and bought a house. A second child, you, was born to the couple in White Eagle in 1990. Legal and financial records in the name of Grant Walton Thomas were filed regularly and consistently until he died in 2003. It's at that point that the paper trail ends. If the man who keeps popping up in photos tagged by my software is your father and not simply a look-alike, he has to be using a different name and identity now."

I took in a deep breath, held it, and then blew it out slowly. "Okay, what do you think? Is my dad a foreign spy? He didn't have an accent or the look of a foreigner. Or do you think he's a fugitive? Could he be in witness protection? Or even an asset of the United States who's so valuable they asked him to sacrifice his family to serve his country?"

"Maybe."

"Maybe to which part?" I asked, frustration evident in my voice.

"Any of it."

I leaned back in my chair and closed my eyes. This search for answers was exhausting. Once again, I had to ask myself if I wanted to go on. "So what now?"

"If you want to continue—and I'm going to suggest you think about that question seriously—I think our next move is to try to track down the private investigator Galvin Kline hired."

"Do you know his name?"

"I didn't when we discussed this before, but I do now. I sweet talked the woman who was Galvin Kline's assistant at the time the photo was taken into telling me who he would have hired to conduct personal and private surveillance. She gave me the name of a firm that turned out not to be involved, but one of the clerks gave me the name of a man who operated under the radar. It took me a while to track him down, but he's living in a small town in Minnesota. He's unwilling to tell me what he considers to be confidential information, but I think I can get him to talk."

"How?" I asked.

Tony glanced at me. "It might be better if you didn't know the details."

I frowned. "You aren't going to hurt him, are you?"

Tony shook his head. "No. At least not physically. Give me some time and we can revisit this again."

"You're going to dig up some dirt on him so you can use it to blackmail him."

Tony raised a brow but didn't respond. I hated to have Tony do anything illegal for me, but I really wanted to know whatever he was concealing. If Kline was trailing the man I suspected was my father, chances were he knew something we didn't. I hoped something would lead to the answers I needed to have the closure I desired.

Chapter 3

Saturday, October 20

I'd been a volunteer for the local animal shelter since I was in high school. Back then, Brady's uncle had owned the veterinary hospital and the shelter, but when Brady bought his uncle's practice last December, he took on the management of the shelter as well. While I thought Brady's uncle had done a wonderful job, Brady has brought a new enthusiasm to the otherwise routine adoption events. In February, we'd had a Valentine's party for the animals that were scheduled for adoption as well as any prospective doggy parents who wanted to attend, and in April, Brady organized a speed-dating event. We don't do a theme clinic every month, but this time we decided to bring some Halloween spirit to the clinic by sponsoring a costume party. While it would have been fun to dress up the dogs, we didn't want to let costumes get in the way of interactions between the animals and their perspective humans, so only the volunteers dressed up. I decided to come as a vampire and Julia, my assistant coordinator, was an evil clown, which was just a bit too creepy if you asked me.

"We have three applications for the Sheltie already," Julia informed me. "They all look good. Perhaps we should remove her from the mix."

"That's fine. Let's see if we can process the applications we already have before the clinic is over. The two families who aren't chosen might want to consider one of the other dogs."

"All three applicants are local. I think any of them would provide a good home."

"Here, let me take a look at those." I held out my hand. The first application was from a woman who taught fifth grade at the elementary school. She was married, and she and her husband owned their own home. They had three children ranging in age between four and ten. I saw no reason not to grant her permission to adopt, but I wasn't sure the Sheltie was the best fit. The second application was from one of the young woman who worked at the local coffee bar.

She was single and lived in an apartment, but I was familiar with her building and knew dogs were allowed. She'd specifically requested a smallish dog with low exercise needs. The Sheltie fit the bill for both; the dog was older and slept a lot. The third application was from a man named Colton, who I knew was now retired but used to work at the local furniture store. He owned his own home, his yard was fenced, and he was looking for a walking partner and companion. He, like the coffee bar employee, had requested a dog on the smaller side.

I turned to Julia. "I agree. All three would provide loving, safe homes. It's my opinion, however, that the first applicant might do better with a younger dog. Not a puppy exactly, but with three kids who are going to want to play with the new family member, a dog as old as the Sheltie might not be the best fit. How about that Border collie Brady just released from quarantine? He's similar in size but quite a bit younger."

"I think the applicant is still here. I'll see if she wants to spend some time with the Border collie."

"Okay, great. As for Colton, he wants a dog he can walk with. Again, I'm not sure the Sheltie is the best fit. I'm not sure of her exact age, and she's very healthy, but I'm willing to bet she's inching into her teens. Let's see if he wants to take a look at the golden mix."

Julia agreed with me there as well. Which left the young woman who worked at the coffee bar with the Sheltie who seemed to prefer napping to almost any other activity.

I sent Julia to talk to the applicants, then went to the exercise area, where people who wanted to spend time with the dogs could walk and play with them. It was a beautiful autumn day. The countryside was brilliant with color as the trees turned bright yellow, orange, and red before shedding their leaves. The local radio station had predicted a storm later in the week, but today was about as perfect a day as you were likely to find at this time of year.

After a while, Colton, the applicant I'd suggested might be better suited for the golden mix, came over to talk to me. "I understand the Sheltie is no longer available."

"I'm so sorry if you had your heart set on her. She's an older dog who isn't likely to want to go on lots of walks. At least not long walks, and you indicated that was one of the reasons you wanted to get a dog."

The man chuckled. "I did say that, and I get that an older dog might not be interested. Most days I'd just as soon skip it myself, but my doctor insists I get more exercise."

"The golden mix is a nice mellow dog who shouldn't demonstrate any behavior problems, and she's a lot more likely to want to get outdoors."

"She does seem like a sweetheart. I didn't think I wanted a dog that big when I came in. I was concerned about being able to control a larger dog on the leash, but she doesn't seem to pull the way the last golden I had did."

"If you'd like, we can do a conditional adoption. Take her home for a few days, and if it doesn't work out, you can bring her back."

The man nodded. "I might just do that. I've been thinking about taking a drive out to the old Harrington place. I guess it might be nice to have a dog along for company."

"Do you know Jordan Westlake?" I asked, curious to find out what, if anything, Colton knew.

"Never met him, but I know he needs some furniture repaired. He called the store where I used to work, and they referred him to me. I don't have the stamina to work full-time anymore, but I still have a woodworking shop in my garage, and I like puttering around with things I pick up at flea markets and yard sales."

"You've lived here a long time. Do you know much about the history of the house?"

Colton nodded his head of white hair. "Sure. I guess most folks who've been around for any amount of time have heard the stories." His blue eyes grew thoughtful. "It was a tragedy really. Such a damn shame."

"My mom told me the oldest daughter went missing almost sixty years ago and was assumed murdered, and the oldest son was shot when he confronted the man he believed had killed his sister."

Colton reached down to pet the head of the dog who was standing quietly beside him. "That much is true. It was a terrible time for the entire community, with everyone wondering if we had a killer in our midst."

I brushed a stray hair from my face. "I heard all five siblings died while living in the house."

"That's true if you assume, as most do, that the daughter was murdered."

"I've been told the youngest son, Houston, jumped from the third story to his death when he was fourteen. He was the last survivor and lived in the house by himself with only a caretaker."

"That much is true too. Never did understand why his father didn't come for him. Doesn't seem right to desert your own kin like that."

I agreed with that. It seemed both strange and wrong. "Do you know what happened to the other two? Their names, I think, were Henrietta and Hannah."

"Henrietta Harrington fell down the stairs and died I guess a couple of years after Hudson was shot. The official cause of death was an accidental fall, but most folks around here thought she was pushed."

"Pushed? By whom?"

Colton shrugged. "Don't know. There were some who thought it was one of the household help, others one of her siblings. No one knew for certain what happened, but everyone suspected there were some strange things going on in that house. There were even some who thought it was the ghost of one of her dead siblings who caused the tumble. Whatever it was, the whole thing was swept under the rug much too quickly."

"What about Mr. Harrington? Did he come when the death occurred? Wouldn't you think a powerful man like that would demand answers?"

Colton shrugged. "Don't rightly remember hearing that he was around, but I was just a young'un then, so everything I heard was secondhand."

"And the others? The mother and Hannah?"

"Mrs. Harrington died shortly after Hudson was shot. Most say she died of a broken heart, but I suspect there may have been more to it than that. That was when a caregiver was brought in to look after the three younger children. The last girl died two years after her sister fell down the stairs, and the youngest child killed himself shortly after that."

"How did the last girl die?"

"Now that's a good question. There was a lot of speculation about what exactly occurred. Some say she got sick and never recovered, while others are certain foul play was involved in her death."

I frowned. "Wasn't there a police investigation?"

Colton shook his head. "No. The family just buried her. I'm not even certain how long she'd been gone before anyone other than those living in the house even knew about it."

"That doesn't sound right."

"I agree. But you need to keep in mind, White Eagle was a tiny little settlement back then, not the booming metropolis it is today."

I raised a brow. White Eagle was far from booming, even today.

Colton went on. "The only law around then was Peter Bennington. He was hired by the merchants in town to keep a level of law and order. Up to then, there hadn't been a budget for law enforcement, so folks took care of things in their own way. When the town, which was just springing up, began to flourish, they hired Bennington. Of course, the Harrington house was outside his jurisdiction. Bennington did look into it when the first daughter went missing, and he followed up when the brother was shot, but other than that, I don't think he had a lot of interaction with the family. When the girl fell down the stairs, the family buried her. When the last girl got sick and died, the family took care of that too."

"So the father of these five children just left them out there in the middle of nowhere to die? That doesn't make sense. What kind of man would do such a thing?"

"An evil man with plans of his own. There was a lot of speculation about the passing of all those Harringtons, but there was no speculation about Hartford Harrington using the house as a dumping ground for the family he'd stopped wanting. I don't know if he ever came back to visit once he left them here. He seemed to take care of them financially. The house surely was a grand one, and I don't remember ever hearing they wanted for money. It could be in his own mind, he thought he was doing for them what the head of a household should. But he must have had a soul of granite to leave those kids here the way he did, even if he had fallen out of love with his wife."

I couldn't agree more. He sounded like a monster, and all the Harrington deaths were suspicious to me. I wouldn't be at all surprised to learn there was a whole lot more going on than anyone at the time knew. I thought of Tony's offer to look into it and decided that was a good idea for sure.

By the time the clinic was over, we'd managed to find humans for all but three of the dogs. Two of them had just been released from quarantine and were likely to find homes within the next few weeks, but the other, an adolescent pit bull mix, had been at the shelter for a while, and I was concerned about his ability to find his own happily ever after. The main problem, I realized, was that he was shy and standoffish, a tough-looking dog that was attractive to some of our male applicants, but when you approached him, he hid and cowered. I had a feeling he'd been abused, but I hoped that with some quality one-on-one time and a bit of retraining, I could help him through the psychological issues he'd been demonstrating. I didn't have time to work with him today, but I didn't think it would hurt to bring him to Tony's, where he could be integrated into a family situation. Maybe Frank would take him if I could nudge him out of his fear and shyness. Frank didn't have a dog, but he seemed to love Tilly. He'd recently bought a house, so I knew he had the room for a dog, should he want one.

I called Tony to ask if it was all right if I brought the dog, who everyone had been calling Pisser because he tended to piss on the floor when nervous, with me for the weekend. Tony was fine with the idea. Because we weren't going to be home that evening to keep an eye on him, Tony suggested we make him a bed in the mudroom, where the tile floor would be easily cleaned if he had an accident.

I called Brady to tell him what I was doing, then brought the dog out to my Jeep. "The first thing we need to do is find you a new name," I said as I made sure he was all tinkled out, then loaded him into the cargo area. "How about Buddy? It's simple and to the point, and it's sure a lot better than Pisser."

Buddy was shaking, I imagined because he was being exposed to a new situation, but when I held out my hand in an offer of comfort, he licked it.

"Okay, Buddy. We need to stop by Hap's to pick up some paint, and then we're going out to Tony's. I won't be at Hap's but for a few minutes, but the drive to Tony's is a long one. It'd be best if you settled in and took it easy. Maybe took a nap. When we get to Tony's, I'll introduce you to Tony, Titan, and Tilly. You'll like them. I'm thinking after you get used to everyone, you'll start to relax a bit. I think we'll wait to introduce you to the cats until tomorrow at least. They can be pushy at times. If I know Tang, he'd probably scare you to death."

I left Buddy in the Jeep while I ran in to pick up Tony's paint. As long as I was there, I bought some orange lights, pumpkin-scented candles, and fake cobwebs for my cabin. The cats would probably shred the cobwebs if I strung them inside, but maybe I'd hang them outside, on my deck. I'd stop at the market later in the week and get some pumpkins as well. When Mike and I were kids, my mom and dad used to take us to a pumpkin patch not far from town, where we'd each pick out our own bright orange gourd to carve a scary face into for Halloween night.

Tony was outside with Titan and Tilly when we arrived at his house, so I had him put the dogs in the house to start, then lifted Buddy out of the Jeep. He was shaking like crazy when I first brought him down, but Tony had a comforting way about him, and before I knew it, Buddy was wagging his tail and following Tony around like a duckling follows its mama.

When Buddy had relaxed a bit, I went inside to shower and change out of my vampire costume while Tony let Tilly into the yard. She's the nurturing sort who finds a way to take care of all the needy animals who come into her life. It took a good thirty minutes before Buddy wanted to play with her, but patience prevailed, and when it was time for Tony and me to get ready for our dinner with Mike and Bree, Buddy was happy and comfortable with all of us. And he was fine being left in the mudroom with food and water, a bed, and some toys. Tomorrow would be soon enough to reexpose him to everything he'd learned to handle today. I figured even if Frank didn't want to adopt him, it would be easier to find the right placement for him once we got him to the point where he was happy and confident and didn't shake and cower over every little thing.

"I think Buddy did really well, and we only had a few hours to work with him," I said to Tony as we drove toward town and Bree's house, where we'd planned to meet.

"I bet he was abused as a pup. He doesn't seem to know who or what he can trust. It's almost like he expects people and experiences to bring him pain. I think it might take a while, but he seems to want to find love and comfort. I think he'll be okay in the long run. Did you have someone in mind for him?"

"Frank. I haven't asked him yet, but he's a good guy, and I can see him having the patience Buddy needs."

"You should ask him to come by the house tomorrow. Introduce them to each other. Maybe if there's a connection between the two, Frank will be willing to work with him the way we did."

I nodded. "Okay. That's a good idea. I'll call him to see if he's open to the idea. If not, I'm sure I can find someone else who'll give Buddy the patience he needs and deserves."

"What about Shaggy?" Tony said.

I frowned. "Shaggy?"

"I know Shaggy seems like a screwup, but he's actually a good guy. He has his own home and a job that would allow him to bring his dog to work. If Frank adopts Buddy, he'll most likely have to leave him home during the day, but Shaggy owns his own business, so that isn't a limitation."

"Do you think Shaggy could take care of a dog? It seems as if he can barely take care of himself."

Tony shrugged. "I know that's how he comes off at times, but remember, his business is successful. If he wasn't conscientious, he'd be out of business. Besides, he can be very nurturing. He really does have a soft jelly center. I'm not saying Frank would be a bad choice, but it seems as if Frank would do better with a dog who could be a partner. Maybe even a trained K-9. Buddy has special needs and requires a certain environment. Being around Shaggy, who's about as kick back as it comes, might be just right for him."

I paused to consider. "Do you think Shaggy would be interested?"

"I think he might. I can ask him. Maybe invite him over tomorrow to meet the pup."

"I haven't talked to Frank yet, so that won't be a problem, and you do make some good points. Shaggy is a fun-loving guy who probably won't freak out if Buddy piddles on his shoe if they happen across something that scares him while out walking. If you think Shaggy will be a responsible pet owner, I'm willing to give it a try."

Tony nodded. "Okay. I'll call him. I think this is going to work out just fine."

Chapter 4

"Are we meeting at Bree's house or at the restaurant?" Tony asked as we headed to town.

"Her house. Mike is going to meet us there as well. We'll probably all drive to the restaurant together. Mike made a reservation, but the parking lot is sure to be full on a Saturday night."

"Seems the restaurant might have provided a larger lot."

I nodded. "Yeah. They need additional space, but I guess the man who built the restaurant only had so much to work with and didn't want to give up any of the square footage inside, so he compromised. A lot of people park on the street now, which is going to be a problem once it starts to snow. By the way, don't let me forget to ask Mike and Bree about the harvest festival. Bree and I usually go together, but with their new state of coupledom, I'm assuming she'll be going with Mike. We can all go together if they want."

"However it works out is fine with me. Are you getting used to Bree and Mike as a couple?" Tony asked.

I paused before answering. "I'm still a little bit concerned the whole thing will blow up and ruin what we've had since childhood, but they seem really happy now, and I want that for them. At first, seeing them kiss or hold hands felt strange, but I'm used to it at this point." I turned slightly in my seat. "Bree thinks I'm overthinking things, and maybe I am, but Mike is my brother and Bree is my best friend. I don't want things to end up weird between them."

"If you want my opinion, I think they have what it takes to make it for the long haul."

I smiled. "I hope so. If it does work out and they get married, Bree will be my sister, which I'd very much welcome. Mom seems to be happy with the arrangement, and so does Bree's mom. I guess I'm the only one who still has reservations, but the more time that passes, the better I feel about things."

"Change can be difficult." Tony took my hand in his. "But it can also open doors to wonderful new experiences, and it's necessary to keep life from becoming stagnant."

"I'm sure you're right, but when you're happy, content with the way things are, spinning the wheel seems like an unnecessary risk."

Tony pulled into Bree's drive and parked. I paused to admire her seasonal decorations, then slipped out of the passenger seat and headed up the walk. I was looking forward to dinner. It had been a while since the four of us had had the opportunity to get together. In the beginning, I think Mike and Bree knew their relationship was freaking me out, so they avoided being together when I was around. By the time I'd begun to get used to their new paradigm, Tony was elbow deep in his project, so he wasn't available to hang out much. I hoped things would even out a bit over the holidays, so I could spend time with all the people who were important to me together.

Mike was already at Bree's, so after we greeted one another, we went out to Bree's sedan, leaving the guys' trucks behind. Mike drove, and Tony and I sat in the back. We'd just pulled into the restaurant's parking lot when Mike got a text from Frank, who was on duty.

"What is it?" Bree asked.

Mike's mouth hardened. "Frank had a call from Jordan Westlake. It seems he found a skeleton in his closet. Literally. I'm sorry, but I need to go. Why don't the three of you go on in and have dinner?"

"It wouldn't be the same without you," I said.

"Besides, we all came together," Bree pointed out. "If you drop us off, we won't have a way to get home if you get held up. We'll just come with you."

"I don't know how long this might take," Mike warned us.

"It's fine," I added. "We'll wait while you do what you have to, and then we can all grab a bite somewhere after."

"I'll call the restaurant and cancel the reservation," Bree offered. "I'm sure they'll understand, given the situation."

Mike hesitated, then agreed.

"So, by skeleton, you mean..." Bree began

"A body," Mike finished.

"Who?" I asked.

Mike shrugged. "I don't know."

"Yeah, but it's been boarded up," I pointed out.

"Maybe, but I'm sure during the past half century there have been squatters who've made use of the shelter it provides," Mike argued.

Mike was probably correct. While I wouldn't want to hole up in a house where so many people had died, White Eagle did have a transient population that came to camp here during the summer, then either left or found shelter during the long, cold winters.

At Harrington House, Mike asked us to wait in the car while he checked out the situation. A few minutes later, he returned and brought us in. The skeleton Jordan Westlake had found wasn't the remains of a recent death but appeared to be at least several decades old. Once Mike introduced us to Mr. Westlake, we were offered seats in the front parlor while Frank and Mike headed up to the attic with him.

Mike had warned us it might be a while, and he was right. "This house is even creepier on the inside than it is on the outside," Bree whispered.

Structurally, I found the house huge but ordinary, although I could see why Bree found it creepy. The structure was sided with dark wood that gave the outside a sinister feeling. The building was big, with three stories of living space, along with an attic and a basement. The small windows were covered with dark shutters, which had been opened since Jordan Westlake arrived, but must have blocked most of the natural light from the interior in the years it had stood empty. If someone had snuck in and found shelter here, it was unlikely anyone would know from the outside.

"It looks like no one has touched a thing since the family lived here," Tony added. "I wonder if there are clothes in the closets and dishes in the kitchen."

"I wonder if there are clues to be found up in the bedrooms," I added.

"Maybe," Tony answered. "Tonight might not be the best time to pursue that line of thought, but maybe we can talk to Mr. Westlake at another time."

"So whose skeleton do you think is stashed in the closet upstairs?" Bree asked us after we'd been waiting for Mike for at least twenty minutes.

I frowned. "I don't know. It seems very odd. If you're going to kill someone, why would you stash them in the closet? Why not just dump the body in the woods or, better yet, bury it in the family cemetery?"

"Maybe the body has been here since the Harringtons lived here. Maybe it belongs to one of those poor kids," Bree said.

"God, I hope one of those kids didn't end up stashed in a closet." I wrinkled my nose.

"I did some research while you were at the clinic today," Tony said to me. "Hartford Harrington built the house in 1955. Over the course of the next four years, his entire family died. I can see why you might suspect the body in the closet is one of them, but based on what I could find out, it seems all their bodies, with the exception of Hillary's, have been accounted for and are buried in the little family plot at the edge of the property."

I raised my brows. "So maybe the body in the closet is Hillary. What if the bloody clothes in the woods were a decoy? What if someone living in this house killed her and then stashed her body?"

"I suppose it's a possibility," Tony answered. "Maybe Mike will have more information when he comes down. If it wasn't Hillary, it's most likely going to be hard to figure out who it was. No one has lived in the house since the last Harrington died. At least not officially. While the skeleton could be Hillary, I think it belonging to a squatter makes more sense."

"It would be so freaky to open a closet and find a skeleton there." Bree shuddered.

"I'd think Jordan Westlake must have prepared himself for a certain amount of freakiness when he made the decision to move into a house so many people believe is haunted," I responded.

"I think the haunted part would bother me less than the tragic reminder of all the people who died while living here," Bree countered.

"It does seem odd there are so many loose threads," Tony added. "The oldest daughter went missing, but her body was never found, unless that skeleton is her. That led to her older brother being shot trying to avenge her death. Then the middle daughter died after a fall down the stairs. The youngest girl died under very mysterious circumstances, although most people say she was ill, and the youngest jumped from the third story of the house. If I was the one who inherited this house, I think the first thing I'd do would be to dig up the answers for the unanswered questions that are just lurking about."

"Maybe Westlake plans to do that," I said.

A few minutes later, Frank came down, went to the front door, and let the coroner in. Both men went upstairs with a body bag. I supposed there wasn't much Mike could do right now. It wasn't as if there were an active crime scene upstairs to secure. Whoever had been waiting in the closet to be found had been there for a very long time. Maybe since before the last Harrington died and the house was locked up for the final time.

******

After Tony and I got back to his place, we took all three dogs out for a walk. We never had gotten around to having dinner. Mike said the coroner was fairly certain the skeleton belonged to an adult female, not a child. If that were true, it most likely wasn't Hillary. However it turned out, Mike wanted to wash up after spending time in the dusty attic, so he dropped us off at Bree's to pick up Tony's truck. They invited us to stay for takeout, but we decided to head back to Tony's, where he'd whip up some omelets after we took out the dogs to stretch their legs.

"Well, that wasn't the evening I expected," I said as they trailed along behind us. But even Buddy seemed happy and relaxed this evening, which did my heart good. Tony had called Shaggy, who said he wanted to meet Buddy, so he was coming over tomorrow.

"Different but interesting," Tony said. "And Jordan Westlake seems really nice."

"I thought so too." Bree, Tony, and I had chatted with him for a few minutes after Mike and Frank escorted the coroner out. He was surprised by his discovery, but not as weirded out as you'd think. In fact, he seemed to be taking everything in stride.

"He was interested in finding out who the body belonged to," Tony added. "Especially when the coroner all but eliminated Hillary."

"I wonder if they can figure that out with what they have to work with. It's not like they can get fingerprints and DNA evidence from a skeleton. I doubt there's anything left of the Harringtons buried outside to match it to, even if they could come up with a sample."

"Unless the skeleton can be connected to a missing person, or there are medical or dental records to match, it will be hard to put a name to the body," Tony agreed.

"Maybe someone who was around back then would be able to provide some insight regarding who, other than Hillary Harrington, might have been missing. Of course, we don't know exactly when *then* is," I added. "Still, the house was built more than sixty years ago. Mrs. Bradford is close to ninety, and I'm pretty sure she's lived here her entire life. She might remember the Harringtons and the goings-on at the time. I could give her a call tomorrow. She was willing to talk to me when I was looking for Patricia Porter."

Tony bent over and gave Titan a rub. "It's worth a try. I was pretty intrigued by the Harrington mystery when you first mentioned it. Then, after I did a bit of research, I was even more interested. Now I'm damn fascinated."

I grinned. "Yeah. Me too."

Tony's pace slowed somewhat as we rounded the end of the small private lake. I looped my arm though his as the dogs settled in around us. "The lights around the house look really nice from back here. I have to say they've inspired me. I bought some lights and a few other decorations to put out at my cabin."

"I can help you hang them tomorrow if you'd like," Tony offered.

"I'd appreciate that. I still need to find some pumpkins for the porch. Did you get yours at the market?"

"No, I got them at the farmers market in Kalispell. I'd say we could run down there and pick some up for you, but I don't think we'll have time. I'm fairly certain the little seasonal nursery south of town is selling pumpkins. We can run over there tomorrow if you'd like."

When the dogs had had their fill of exercise, we headed back inside, and I fed all the animals while Tony whipped up the omelets and toast. Not the gourmet meal I'd been expecting when we'd set out for dinner tonight but delicious, especially after the crazy evening we'd had.

"What else did you dig up on the Harringtons while I was at the clinic this morning?" I asked as we ate.

"I ran out of time to look too deeply, but I pulled the report for Hillary Harrington's disappearance. There was an adequate if not inspired investigation. The man in charge could have done a lot more to follow up on leads that initially didn't seem to go anywhere, but I can't say anything was swept under the rug, as some residents at the time seemed to think."

I took a bite of my cheesy omelet, chewed, and swallowed. "It does seem as if Hillary's disappearance set off the series of events that escalated as time went by, and the fact that the father didn't come for his children is, in my opinion, the oddest thing of all. I think there's a story to uncover."

"I agree. And now that I've finished my project and have some extra time on my hands, I'm willing to do some more investigating. You in?" Tony asked.

"I'm in. We were supposed to play video games tonight, but how about we clean up here, then head downstairs? We should come up with a list of questions to ask Mrs. Bradford. She might be willing to meet with us tomorrow, and I want to be ready to get the most from our conversation."

"Researching all the deaths while the Harringtons lived in that house might waylay us. I suggest we focus on Hillary's disappearance, then see where that leads us."

It felt wrong to be excited by the idea of investigating the probable murder of a young girl, but I was. It felt good to be back in the thick of a mystery with Tony again. Digging for facts and developing theories really was a rush if you allowed yourself to admit it.

The first thing Tony did was pull up the report of Hillary Harrington's disappearance he'd hacked into earlier in the day. As we knew, she was fourteen when she moved with her mother and siblings to Harrington House. According to statements obtained at the time, she hadn't been happy about the move and was resentful that she'd had to leave her school and friends behind. While the other Harrington offspring seemed to have gone along with their father's wishes, Hillary acted out in a loud and forceful manner. Not only did she sneak out of the house on numerous occasions, but when she made her way into town, she made sure that anyone who would listen knew what a monster her father was for destroying her life and the lives of her brothers and sisters.

I guess I could understand why she was so upset. To be torn from her world and isolated with only her siblings for company had to have been unimaginably difficult. For the life of me, I couldn't imagine why the girl's father would have done such a thing. No matter how many different ways I tried to look at it, the move seemed cruel and unnecessary. Frankly, I was surprised to find that Hillary was the only Harrington to have acted out over it.

"I wonder if a boy was involved," I murmured, interrupting as Tony went through the notes he'd taken. "Hillary went to bed and then snuck off during the night. Her bloody clothes were found in the woods the next morning. Sneaking off alone after dark seems to me to be the sort of thing a girl looking to hook up with a guy would do."

"That was considered an option," Tony answered. "From the interviews conducted, if she was meeting a boy, no one knew who he might be. Of course, it also tracks that she might have kept that information to herself. From what I've gathered, her father wasn't at all happy to find out she'd been going around town bad-mouthing him. One teen said Hillary's father had hired a man not only to help out with household repairs but to make sure Hillary stayed locked up in the house."

I frowned. "What man? Is there a name?"

Tony looked at his notes. "It just says a man. I haven't found any other references to a man hired by Hillary's father, so the report might not even have been accurate. The one really consistent thing I've found is that the interviews were spotty. It appears information may be missing."

"I had a chat with a man named Colton at the clinic today. He told me White Eagle hadn't been incorporated back then and was little more than some residences and businesses that had sprung up from the lumber operation in the area. According to him, there was only one person, Peter Bennington, who was hired to enforce the law, and he focused on crimes that took place closer to the little settlement where most of the people lived. Harrington House must have seemed even farther from town back then. Maybe he did a perfunctory search before moving on to crimes closer to the area he was hired to protect."

"I guess it might have happened that way. Still, Hartford Harrington was a rich and powerful man. I would think he'd have pushed for answers, but apparently, he didn't."

The more I learned about Hartford Harrington, the less I liked him. He sounded like a sociopath who seemed to have decided he no longer wanted his family, so he'd stashed them away where they wouldn't interfere with his life. What a scumbag. "Okay, go on. What else do you have?" I asked after I tamped down my anger just a bit.

Tony returned his attention to the computer screen and took a minute to look at his notes. "As we know, Hudson Harrington thought Wilbur Woodbine was responsible for Hillary's disappearance. He said Wilbur lived on the adjoining property, and for reasons he didn't fully understand, Hillary took a liking to him. Hudson caught her sneaking off to visit Wilbur, a man in his twenties, on several occasions. Hudson was aware that his sister wanted to punish everyone around her for disrupting her life, and he made the leap to there being more than friendship going on."

I made a face. "Did he think they were having an affair?"

"Not in the strictest sense. From what Hudson said to others, it seemed he thought they were doing things a grown man shouldn't be doing with a child."

"Did he have any proof? I mean, more than just a hunch?" I asked.

"Not that I could find. But that was a very long time ago, and I don't have a record of Hudson's actual thoughts about the matter. All I found was speculation and secondhand accounts of conversations."

"So Hudson confronted Woodbine and was shot and killed."

Tony nodded. "Wilbur never wavered from his insistence that he didn't have an inappropriate relationship with Hillary. He said she was an angry and lonely child who sometimes came over to his place to complain about her life. He'd listen and offer sympathy, but that, he said, was the extent of it."

I furrowed my brow. "I suppose it could have been that way, but I can also understand why Hillary's brother might have had a problem with her having a secret relationship with a grown man. The whole thing feels hinky."

"I don't disagree."

I tried to put myself in the mind of a fourteen-year-old adolescent who had basically had her entire life pulled out from under her. I couldn't even imagine how devastating that would be. Fourteen was such a difficult age anyway, but to feel imprisoned by your own father for no apparent reason? At least I didn't know of a reason. I just didn't get it. "Who else was looked at regarding Hillary's disappearance?"

"No one," Tony answered. "Other than Wilbur, no one else stood out as a suspect. You have to remember, there was no real police force in town, just one man paid to keep the peace. The family was new to the area, and other than Hillary, who snuck out on a fairly regular basis, the others seemed to honor the father's request to remain at home, so they didn't know many people. There was no physical evidence other than the bloody clothing found in the woods, and nothing to link anyone to Hillary's disappearance. This Bennington hit a dead end and moved on."

"Who found the bloody clothes?" I asked.

"Hudson. When she wasn't in her room and no one could find her in the house, he set out on his bike to look for her. She'd wandered off into the woods behind the house before, so he went there and found her clothing about halfway between Harrington House and Wilbur Woodbine's home."

As much as I enjoyed a mystery to research, I was hating this one. A fourteen-year-old most likely had been murdered with no one knowing how it happened, and her older brother, who believed she'd been murdered by their neighbor, was killed trying to avenge her death.

"So what now?" I asked. "Hillary disappeared so long ago. It's going to be hard to pick up any threads now."

Tony nodded. "It's going to be tough unless someone saw something."

"I'll call Mrs. Bradford tomorrow and take it from there. I assume Peter Bennington is dead?"

Tony nodded. "I have his notes, but whatever else he knew or suspected died with him. A lack of witnesses is true of most mysteries that are never solved. Anyone who might know the facts dies off, leaving only those who base their theories on tidbits of information that more often than not don't or can't form a clear picture. But we've been in this situation before and things came out okay. Maybe we'll be lucky again."

I hoped Tony was right. I didn't suppose there was anyone left alive who much cared if the mystery was solved or not. The story of Hillary's disappearance had gone unanswered for so long, anyone who would have known her was probably dead. I thought of her father and wonder again why he had dumped his family here, why he hadn't responded with help when things began to go south. Was it possible he was somehow involved? I guess the fact he was in San Francisco while his family was here made it unlikely. But there was definitely something wrong about the family. Maybe the father had grown tired of Hillary's rebellion and hired someone, as was speculated, to keep her in line. Maybe she'd resisted and things had become violent. Again, I didn't see how we could determine the likelihood of any of our theories at this late date, but I was still interested in trying to find answers that might very well be buried forever.

I glanced at Tony, who was frowning at his computer screen. "What is it?" I asked.

"I was checking my email before we turned in."

"And…?"

"And someone sent me a photo of a woman standing on what looks to be the same bridge Jared Collins was on in the other photo."

"The bridge in Norway?"

Tony nodded.

"Do you know who the woman is?"

"I think it's your mother."

Chapter 5

Sunday, October 21

My head had been spinning since the moment Tony had told me the woman in this new photo looked an awful lot like my mother. This woman was young; I doubted she was more than twenty, if that. She had blond hair, while my mother's hair was dark, and she was wearing large sunglasses, so it was impossible to see her eye color. I'd wanted to call my mother at that very moment to confront her, but Tony had pointed out that it was almost midnight, my mom would most likely be asleep, and we didn't know for certain the photo was of her despite the similarity. I finally agreed a conversation with Mom could wait for daybreak. Of course, what that really translated to was me spending the entire night imagining every possible scenario when I should have been sleeping. Was my mom a spy of some sort, as I had begun to imagine was true of my father? Had Dad needed to disappear while Mom had to stay, which led to his fake death? Was Romero Montenegro really her much younger lover, or was he a spy too, who had been spending time with her in some official capacity? The questions went on and on.

And then I spent a good hour trying to remember if Mom had ever mentioned visiting Norway. I didn't remember her saying she had, but I also didn't remember her saying she hadn't. Unlike my father, who had specifically said he'd never been to Europe, I was fairly sure the subject had never come up.

Tony thought it was a bad idea to shove the photo in front of Mom's face and demand answers, which I was inclined to do, so I started with a call to my Aunt Ruthie. If my mother had ever gone overseas, surely her sister would know about it.

"Hi, Aunt Ruthie," I said after I felt I'd waited long enough into the morning not to wake her. "It's Tess. I hate to bother you, but I'm doing one of those family tree things and have a few questions."

"I'd be happy to tell you what I know, and I'd love to see the results of your family tree. I've been meaning to do one but haven't found the time."

Great. Knowing Ruthie, she'd keep asking about it, so I'd really have to do one. Maybe I should have come up with a less time-consuming lie. "I'm at the part where it asks about relations in other places. You know, like in Europe. Do you know if we have relatives in other countries?"

"I imagine we do. Most folks do, if you look back far enough. But if you're asking if there's anyone I can identify by name, the answer is no. I think at least part of our family comes from France. And possibly Italy. I'm really excited to see what you find out."

"Yeah," I agreed. "It is, although I'm only just getting started. On another note, have you or anyone in our family traveled to Europe?"

"Does it ask that?" Ruthie asked.

"No, but doing the research has made me curious."

"I see. I've never been to Europe. Grandma and Grandpa talked about going, but they never made it over either. I'm pretty sure the only member of our immediate family to make the trip is your mom."

My eyes grew big. "My mom?"

"I'm sure she must have told you about the trip she took after high school. She went with a friend. Darla, I think, was her name. She was there for six weeks, or maybe it was eight weeks. It was so long ago, it's hard to remember now. Between you and me, something happened on that trip your mother never wanted to talk about. I'm guessing it was a vacation romance. Whatever it was, she took it hard. When she got home, she didn't want to share the details of her trip. It must have ended up being a painful memory. I suppose that's why she doesn't bring it up. She must have stored it away with her keepsakes. I'd say you should ask her, but she's pretty down about Romero, so it might not be the best time to bring it up."

"I'll tread lightly. Thanks for sharing what you remembered."

"Anytime, honey. Anytime. Now, you be sure to tell me what you find out about our ancestors. I'm very excited to hear."

"Yeah. I will. And thanks again." I hung up my phone, put my hands on my head, and groaned.

"Is something wrong?" Tony who had just walked in from the outdoor deck where he'd been watering his herbs, asked.

"I have to do a family tree."

Tony raised a brow. "A family tree?"

I explained what I'd discovered, along with the potentially time-consuming lie I'd told to get it.

"So, if your mother went to Europe out of high school, she might have gone to Norway. It doesn't explain who took the photo or why it showed up in my in-box, though. Had she met your father yet then?"

"No. She didn't meet Dad until she'd been out of school a year or two. I think she was around twenty or twenty-one. If she'd just graduated high school she would have been around eighteen when the photo was taken."

"So, we have a photo of your mom standing on the same bridge as Jared Collins at about the same time, despite the fact that if he's your father, as we suspect, they wouldn't meet for at least a couple of years. Can that be a coincidence?"

I leaned forward and let out another loud groan. "When you put it that way, it seems unlikely." After a minute, I added, "So what now? Do I talk to my mom? Do I ask her about her trip?"

"I think it might be okay to ask about the trip. Your Aunt Ruthie did mention it to you. I'm not sure I'd bring up the photo, though. She would wonder where you got it, and that might open up a whole other can of worms. Maybe you can just ask her if she has photos from the trip, if you can see them."

"I could do that, although Ruthie thought asking Mom about a trip she took to Europe might not be a good idea while she's mooning over Romero."

Tony sat down next to me. "Maybe you could put a spin on it, mention the family tree, which it now sounds like we'll have to create. Tell your mom you spoke to Ruthie, who brought up her trip. Be up front about your hesitation to ask about it because she's upset over the situation with Romero, but that you're curious and would like to hear about it when she's ready. Maybe she'll want to share her memories."

I leaned back in my chair and stretched my legs out in front of me. "Maybe. But Ruthie said Mom came back from her trip upset. She didn't want to talk about it. Ruthie thought Mom might have had a vacation romance that ended badly. If she's angsty over Romero, she might not want to talk about a trip when some other guy broke her heart."

Tony shrugged. "If she doesn't want to talk about it, she'll tell you so."

I decided to take the risk and called my mom. She was happy to hear from me and hoped I'd be stopping by. It was Sunday, after all, and we'd gotten away from our family dinners because everyone seemed to be so busy lately. I told her I couldn't stay for dinner, but I'd bring lunch to her place. We could eat on her patio and catch up a bit. I didn't tell her what I wanted to know or why. I figured I'd spring that on her when I got there.

Shaggy was coming over in a little while to meet Buddy, and Tony assured me that he'd do everything in his power to make sure the meet and greet went off without a hitch. Initially, I'd thought Shaggy a questionable choice, but the more I thought about it, the more Tony's suggestion seemed right on. Shaggy could take Buddy to work with him, and he was an easygoing guy who wouldn't get upset if Buddy had a few emotional and bladder issues to work through.

******

Mom and I settled on her deck with our lunch and I let her steer the conversation for a while. She asked about my work and the remodel on my cabin, and I asked about her plans for the upcoming holiday season. Eventually, she brought things around to the point. "So, what's really on your mind?" Mom asked. "We see each other almost every day. We've already talked about the holidays. I don't think that's why you're here."

I took a deep breath in, then blew it out slowly. "You're right. I'm here because of a conversation I had with Aunt Ruthie about family trees."

Mom looked confused. "Family trees?"

I nodded. "I've decided to do one. Tony's going to help me. I asked Aunt Ruthie about our ancestors, especially ancestors we had who might still live in other countries. She said she didn't know of any but would be interested in learning about our heritage when we find anything out. One thing led to another, and she mentioned you'd been to Europe after you graduated high school." I paused and looked at her. "It seems a trip to Europe would be sort of a big deal, but I didn't remember you ever talking about it, so I guess I got curious."

Mom didn't say anything right away, which made me feel like squirming. There was a thoughtful look on her face, although she didn't seem particularly upset.

"I know this might not be the best time to ask, with what's been going on with Romero," I added. "If you don't want to talk about it, I understand."

Mom shook her head. "No. It's fine. Romero and I are, or I guess I should say were, just friends. I'm upset he hasn't been in touch, but he has nothing to do with my summer abroad."

"Aunt Ruthie said you didn't like to talk about it."

Mom smiled, a tired little smile. "I don't. Or at least I didn't. Don't get me wrong: the trip was wonderful. The best time in my life. But I was young and acted on impulse then, rather than logic. I knew I was going to have to come home at the end of the trip, but that didn't stop me from falling for a man I met in Norway."

My heart started to pound. "Norway?"

Mom nodded. "Beautiful country. You really should visit sometime."

"And this man you fell in love with lived in Norway?" She had just said as much, but I was so shocked to immediately be getting the answers I wanted, I found myself asking again.

Mom nodded again. "His name was Jared, and I fell for him hard the first time I met him. He was handsome and educated. Cultured and so very funny. He was romantic and thoughtful, and his eyes..." Mom put her hand to her chest. "His eyes were piecing. I know that sounds like a cliché, but his really were. I felt like he could look right through me to my soul."

"You loved him."

Mom bowed her head. "I did. So very much. And he loved me; I was sure of it. But I lived here and he lived there, so we parted. We knew we didn't have a future together, so we just ended it rather than suffering through a long-drawn-out, long-distance thing that would eventually end anyway. It was the worst time of my life."

"Worse than when Dad died?"

Mom huffed out a breath. "Will you think less of me if I say yes? Of course I loved your father, but we never had what Jared and I had. In fact, if I'm totally honest, I think the reason I started dating your dad in the first place was because he looked like Jared. Jared had a way about him that made him seem more handsome than Grant, but other than the hard edges I associate with your father, the two could have been doubles. Though once you got past the physical resemblance, the similarities ended. Your dad was a good man. He provided for his family and he worked hard. But he was difficult to get to know. It was almost as if there was a part of him I could never reach. A part he kept secret. I honestly don't know if we would have lasted if he hadn't been a trucker. He was away most of the time. It was easier that way."

Wow. Did that ever explain a lot.

"Do you have a photo of Jared?" I wondered.

Mom nodded. "I do. Wait here. I'll fetch my shoebox."

I tried not to freak out while I waited. This explained why Mom was on the same bridge as Jared, and why a man looked like my father but had a different name. I wondered why he was being investigated by the state senator and what had happened to him. He obviously wasn't my father. If Mom had loved one man and married the other, there was no way he was the same person. A woman in love would know that.

"Here we go," Mom said.

I took the box and opened it.

"You had blond hair," I said, holding up a photo.

"For a while after high school. I was feeling adventurous and decided to give blond a try. I eventually decided it wasn't for me, changed it back, and have kept it dark ever since."

I continued to look through the box, which was full of photos from her trip. There were photos of her with another girl her age who must have been her friend. There were photos of scenery and photos of Jared. I wanted to show them to Tony, but I didn't want to be obvious about it, so I asked for a drink, then quickly took several photos that showed Jared's face the most clearly and sent them to Tony. Now that I could see Jared's full face, it was clear that while he had some features similar to my father's, there were differences as well.

Mom and I visited for another hour before I made my excuses and left. I wasn't sure if I'd taken a step forward or a step back when it came to figuring out what had happened to my dad. When we thought he and Jared were the same person, I'd felt we had an avenue of investigation. Now I wasn't so sure. I needed to talk to Tony, who I knew would help me make sense of all this.

Chapter 6

Tony had already had a chance to look at the photos I'd sent him by the time I got to his house. We agreed that now that we knew for a fact Jared Collins wasn't my father, it might be best to stop investigating him and focus our attention on finding my dad. We still had the Harrington family mystery to look in to too. I'm not sure why we got wrapped up in mysteries the way we did, but every now and then something came along that spoke to our natural curiosity.

"Doing a family tree isn't a bad idea, you know," Tony said. "It might help us figure out where your father came from."

"Yes, it's still a big question mark. Okay. I'm sort of committed anyway. Where do we start?"

"They have ancestry sites on the internet. Doing your family tree through one of them might be a good idea, in case one of your other family members decides to become involved. I could help you with the research, but if we did everything on our own, we wouldn't be as easily able to let others benefit from what we find." Tony pulled up a site on his computer. "Here's one that has a good reputation. You'll just need to fill out the information and send for a test kit."

I worked on that while Tony did something else. I created an account and sent for the test kit, then turned my attention to him. "So, was Shaggy here to meet Buddy? I became so focused on what I learned from Mom, I didn't think to ask when I first arrived."

"He was here, and he's definitely interested in Buddy. He had to help a friend move some furniture, but he's coming back when he's done. He wants to take Buddy for a trial. I said I'd have to talk to you about it, but I thought it could be worked out."

"I'll call Brady to let him know what we're doing, but that should be fine. We have an extra leash, dog bed, toys, and food he can borrow, so he won't have to buy anything. How did Buddy seem when he met Shaggy?"

"Cautious. Of course, he's always cautious. But Shaggy threw a ball, which drew Titan and Tilly in right away, and eventually, Buddy joined in. I think they'll get along fine once they get to know each other. If they don't, you can always move on to plan B."

"True, and thank you for suggesting Shaggy. The more I think about it, the more certain I am this will work out just fine." I sat down next to Tony. "What are you working on?"

"The Harrington family tragedies. Specifically, Hillary's disappearance. I feel as if that's the catalyst for everything that happened afterward. Did you ever call Mrs. Bradford? You were going to ask her if she remembered anything about the Harringtons."

"I haven't yet, but I will. Maybe she can see us this afternoon."

******

Bella Bradford lived in a cheery house that had wonderful curb appeal. I didn't know her exact age and wasn't inclined to ask, but my best guess was somewhere in her late eighties or early nineties, so that would put her in her twenties when Hillary Harrington disappeared. Certainly old enough to remember it, and to have some opinion of what had gone on at the time.

"Yes, of course I remember when that girl went missing," Bella said after she'd shown Tony and me in and offered us iced tea. "The family hadn't lived in the area long. Maybe a few months. I hadn't met or spoken to any of them, but I remember feeling devastated by what happened. I was newly married and didn't have any children of my own, but my compassion for the mother of that child was profound."

"I understand her body was never found and no suspect in her disappearance was ever identified?"

Bella shook her head. "The case wasn't solved. The oldest boy was sure Wilbur Woodbine killed his sister and hid her body. It was such a shock to an already fragile community when the boy was shot and killed just a short time afterward. I guess I can understand why he suspected Wilbur. He lived alone out there in the woods, just beyond the ravine where the girl's clothing was found. The rumor was that Hillary had befriended him. Everyone knew he wasn't quite right in the head."

"Right in the head?" I asked. This was the first time anyone had described Wilbur as challenged in any way.

"He was a simple man of limited intelligence, although he managed to support himself even though he never finished his schooling."

"Did Mr. Woodbine continue to live here after the disappearance?"

Bella nodded. "Right up until the day he died, which was about twenty years ago, I suppose."

"Do you think he killed Hillary Harrington?" Tony asked.

Bella paused before answering. "No, I don't. Wilbur didn't have the same intelligence and education as his peers, but he wasn't a violent man. The family had just moved to the area and Hudson Harrington couldn't have known the man well, but Wilbur was peaceful. The sort an unhappy teenager might be drawn to if she was looking for a sympathetic ear."

"Do you have a theory of what might have happened to her?" I wondered.

"I don't know what happened to the child, but I will say there was something odd going on with that family from the beginning. The very thought that the father of five children would build a fancy house in the middle of nowhere and abandon them there, never to return, is unimaginable. What kind of a man must he have been to walk away from his family without a second look?"

"So he never came back after the girl went missing?" Tony verified.

"Not as far as I know. Can you imagine such a thing?"

"Were there others living in the house?" I asked. "Household staff?"

Bella nodded. "A few. I remember hearing about a woman who was brought in to cook and clean, as well as a man who helped out with household chores and repairs. The children didn't attend school, but a woman from town went to the house to tutor them. And of course, after Mrs. Harrington died, a nanny was brought in for the three surviving children."

"The children didn't attend school?" I asked. This was a new piece of information. I wasn't certain it was relevant, but it seemed as if it might be.

"No. The children were kept isolated out there in the house. The rumor was that there was something wrong with them, that that was why Mr. Harrington hid them out there in the woods. I don't know if that had any basis in reality. I never spoke to any of the children, but I glimpsed them from a distance from time to time. They looked normal enough."

This was becoming more and more absurd. Why would a rich, powerful man like Hartford Harrington move his entire family to an isolated spot over a thousand miles away from where they lived? Why would he isolate the children by providing a tutor rather than allowing them to attend school? And finally, why would he seemingly ignore everything that went on after he left them?

"The tutor who came to see to the education of the Harrington children," Tony began. "Do you know who that was?"

"Rena Wiggins. She was a young woman, just out of school herself. She moved here shortly before accepting the position."

"Does she still live here?" I asked.

"No. She moved away at some point. I can't remember when exactly."

"Did she own a home?" Tony asked.

"No. She lived in one of those little apartments over by the lake. The ones with the big front porches."

"The Patio Garden Apartments," I supplied.

Bella nodded. "Yes. Those are the units. They were brand-new back then. In fact, I think they were built right around the same time the Harringtons arrived."

I had a friend from school who'd lived in those apartments, which is how I knew Mrs. Watson, the current owner, who was the daughter of the woman who'd owned them when they were first built. Now I wondered if Mrs. Watson remembered Rena Wiggins and had some idea where she went when she left White Eagle. When Tony and I finished here, I'd call her.

"What about the other deaths?" I asked. "By the time Henrietta Harrington fell down the stairs, they'd been living here for a couple of years, and Hannah and Houston Harrington must have lived here about four years before they died. Do you remember there being any speculation about what happened to them?"

"No one said a word when the young girl fell down the stairs," Bella answered. "I'm not even certain anyone was called in to investigate. I know I had no idea what occurred until someone mentioned there were now three graves in the family cemetery."

I supposed the three would have been Hudson, Henrietta, and their mother. "So you don't think Mr. Bennington was called when Henrietta fell?" I clarified.

"No, I don't believe so. I imagine the family took care of things themselves. It wasn't unheard of for wealthy families with their own cemeteries on their land to do so back then."

"What about the staff?" Tony asked. "They must have known what happened. Wouldn't one of them have said something to someone?"

"Perhaps they did. It's possible I just never heard about it."

As soon as we left Bella's, I called Mrs. Watson, who did remember Rena Wiggins. She said she believed she was still alive and lived in Woods Bay. That wasn't all that far away, so I called the number Mrs. Watson gave me and asked to speak to her.

******

Woods Bay was a tiny town focused on recreation about forty miles from White Eagle on the eastern shore of Flathead Lake. Rena Wiggins lived with her daughter and son-in-law in a nice home on a wooded lot. She invited Tony and me to sit out on the patio, where we could speak privately.

"Yes, of course I remember working for the Harringtons," she said after we'd settled in and Tony had launched the conversation. She was an attractive woman who seemed to have a lot of energy given her age. I'd learned that after she'd left Harrington House, she'd taught high school in Missoula for over thirty years. After her husband died, her daughter invited her to move in with her and her husband. "It was my first teaching job after graduating high school. When I got it, I considered myself quite lucky. I wasn't sure I would even qualify for such a high-paying position, but the man who interviewed me didn't seem to care that I was young and hadn't been to college yet. He gave me the idea that was a plus, that I was exactly what they were looking for. I'll tell you, during those first days, I was on cloud nine. Of course, by the end of my time with the family, I had quite a different view of things."

"Perhaps you can tell us what you remember from your time with the family," I said.

She folded her hands in her lap after picking an invisible piece of lint from her dark slacks. "All right. I'll try. It was so long ago."

"Anything at all you can remember might help," I said persuasively.

She looked nervous. Perhaps requesting that she revisit what had to have been a difficult time was a lot to ask.

"Let's see. I started working for the family just a week or so after they moved in. The move had been a huge adjustment for all the children, so I was challenged with trying to find a way into their lives despite the somber mood of the entire household. Hillary was the rebellious one and wanted nothing to do with me or any of the servants, and Hudson was sixteen and not at all interested in receiving instruction from someone who was just two years older than he was. I found the three younger children delightful after a brief period of adjustment. The house was dark and depressing. You could almost sense evil waiting in the shadows. I know that sounds strange, but the house never seemed normal."

"You felt that from the beginning?" I asked. "Even before Hillary went missing and Hudson was shot and killed?"

She nodded. "The house seemed to have its own energy. A negative energy that caused goose bumps on my arms whenever I was alone. I almost quit several times during my first week, but I could see the younger children were happy I was there. They seemed to want to spend time with me. They had a difficult life, and I felt I helped in some way, so I hung in despite my trepidation."

"So you provided lessons for the younger three Harringtons," I confirmed.

"Yes. Not only did I tutor them in the academic areas I'd been instructed to by the man who had hired me, but we spent time doing other things as well."

"What sorts of things?" Tony asked.

"We took hikes when we could get out. The children weren't allowed in town, but at times it was all right with the staff if we took walks in the woods surrounding the house. When we couldn't do that, we made do with the resources we found indoors. We read books and acted out scenes. We played games and worked on the art projects all three of the children enjoyed. I felt I brought an element of normalcy to a very abnormal situation. When I wasn't with them, I suspect the house was a dark and depressing place indeed."

"Other than Mrs. Harrington and the servants you already mentioned, were there other adults on the premises?" Tony asked.

"A cook. She was a nice enough woman, but she kept to herself, rarely leaving the kitchen. There was also a man who helped out with some chores and acted as sort of a guard. I suspected Mr. Harrington hired him to try to control Hillary and left after she disappeared."

"Let's talk about that," I said. "I understand Hillary's clothing was found in the woods behind the house."

She angled her head. "Yes. As I've already said, Hillary was a bit of a wild child. She was just so very angry. I guess I didn't blame her. It had to be very hard for her when she was forced to leave her home and her friends only to be hidden away in a big old house in the middle of nowhere. I know she snuck out despite her father's attempts to control her. I don't know why she ran away or if that's what happened. It did enter my mind that her guard might have grown weary of the struggle and ended Hillary's rebellion once and for all. I know she ran that poor man ragged. Every time she got away and slipped into town, he would get an earful from Mr. Harrington."

"Was he ever looked at as a suspect in Hillary's disappearance?" Tony wondered.

"I don't think so. He only worked at the house for a short time. He left days after Hillary went missing."

That did sound suspicious. I wondered if Bennington had investigated him. His notes should tell us that.

"Was he replaced?" I asked.

"No. At least, no one was brought in to fill his exact job. Mrs. Harrington died shortly after Hillary went missing and Hudson was shot and killed. That was when a nanny was brought in to see to the three younger children."

"And how did that go? Did the children like her?"

She shook her head. "Not at all. She was a cold and very structured woman, and she was put in charge of the whole household. The children hated her, and I'm afraid the two of us didn't get along. I tried to be an advocate for the children when she made unreasonable demands of them but was always immediately overruled. It was a very dark time for everyone in the house."

"Okay, now Hillary is missing, both Hudson and Mrs. Harrington are dead, the guard is gone, and a nanny has been brought in. Then what happened?" I asked.

"After a bit, the remaining children seemed to adjust to the situation. The nanny was a truly nasty woman, but the kids learned to adapt to her ways and I made a point to spend as much time with them as I could. It wasn't ideal, but we managed to make it work—until Henrietta came down with the sickness."

"The sickness? What sickness?" I asked.

"The sickness that caused Henrietta's strange behavior."

"Can you be more specific?" I asked.

She nodded. "I can try, but I'm not an expert on such things."

"That's fine," Tony said. "Just start at the beginning and tell us what you remember."

"Shortly after Henrietta's fourteenth birthday, she began to change. She went from being a pleasant and agreeable child to acting oddly almost overnight."

"Oddly how?" I asked.

"For one thing, she started talking to herself. Not in the absentminded way we all do from time to time when we're trying to work something out. She tried to hide it when she was with the others, but I'd hear her in her room having entire conversations with someone. At first, I thought she might have made a friend she'd snuck in—friends weren't allowed on the property—but after a while I realized the only friend with her was the one in her head."

"An imaginary friend?" I said.

She shrugged. "Perhaps. She seemed a bit old for that, though. The talking to herself was the first symptom, but not the most disturbing."

"Okay," Tony said. "What else was going on?"

"She became paranoid. She started carrying a knife for protection. It was only a butter knife and I didn't think she would actually hurt anyone, but it was still very odd. I tried to talk to her about it, to assure her that she wasn't in any danger, but she insisted there were people in the house. Other people. People I couldn't see. She warned me that those people were dangerous. That they wanted to hurt us, and that we needed to be careful."

"Did you tell anyone about this?" Tony asked.

"I tried to talk to the nanny about it, but she just stared at me with a blank look on her face that seemed to indicate she thought I was crazy. I called Mr. Valdez, the man who first hired me. He assured me that Henrietta was a normal girl with an overactive imagination. He also suggested that the hormones associated with puberty might have something to do with her odd behavior. I was young and willing to admit I didn't know a thing about what can only be described as mentally unstable behavior, so I let him convince me that everything would be fine. But things weren't fine. As time went on, Henrietta's paranoia started manifesting itself in violent behavior. Not necessarily toward anyone else in the household, but she started doing things like hitting walls and throwing things. When I found out that she had fallen down the stairs, I was saddened but not all that surprised. The poor girl had grown reckless. There was no doubt in my mind that she had been running from or chasing a foe only she could see when she slipped and fell."

"So you don't think she might have been pushed?" I asked.

"Pushed? I don't know. I suppose it's possible. Although the only people allowed in that house were family members and a handful of staff. I wasn't there when it happened, so I can't say for certain, but a slip and fall brought on by paranoia seems more likely in my mind. Still, I could imagine Henrietta and the nanny could have become involved in an altercation. Initially, Henrietta tried to hide her odd behavior from the woman. I don't think she wanted word to get back to her father. But as time went on, and Henrietta's psychosis began to take over, things like voices in her head were harder to hide." She glanced toward the house. "I could use a drink. Would you like something? Iced tea? A cola?"

"Maybe some water," I said.

I couldn't help but notice that when she came back with water for Tony and me and a cola for herself, it smelled an awful lot like rum.

"So after Henrietta died," Tony eventually said, "what happened after that?"

"Everyone was sad, but eventually life went on and Hannah, Houston, and I settled in to a somewhat normal routine. About a year later, the nanny and I had a falling out when I tried to convince her to allow the children to be allowed outings away from the house. She was quite adamant that Mr. Harrington wanted them to stay put, and I started to make some noise about emotional abuse. In the end, the nanny won the argument and I was let go. It was a difficult time for me. I worried so about the twins. Unfortunately, my worry seemed to have been justified. Hannah died less than a year after I was fired, and poor Houston went shortly after that." She wiped a tear from her eye. "At least now they can all rest in peace."

Chapter 7

Tony and I drove back to White Eagle in silence. The story Rena Wiggins had told us was heart-wrenching to say the least. It must have been awful to have grown up in that house of horrors. I wondered if Jordan Westlake had any idea what he'd walked into.

"What did you think of her?" I asked Tony.

Tony frowned. "I'm not sure. On one hand, she seemed to exhibit genuine affection for the Harrington children, especially the three younger ones, but her story seemed choppy. It was almost as if she intentionally left things out. Or maybe it was that she felt the need to change facts for some reason."

"So you think she was lying?"

"Not lying exactly. It was more like she was being selective in what she told us. I guess that might just be a normal reaction to being questioned by two people she'd never met before today, bringing back a subject that was deeply emotional for her."

"I suppose it might be that," I agreed. "The entire thing with Henrietta is just too strange. Do you think there was something in the house that made her sick? Something that made her go crazy?"

"Probably not. I won't go so far as to say there's no way the house or something in it could have caused the odd behavior, but I'd be willing to bet there was something else going on. When we get back to my house, I'm going to look in to Hartford Harrington's background. It seems to me he almost knew what was going to happen before it did."

"You think he knew it was possible his family might exhibit symptoms of some sort of mental illness? Something hereditary? Something he knew was coming, so he locked his family away before it could affect him?"

Tony nodded. "That would be my guess. But I feel like there are some missing pieces. I'm hoping some good, old-fashioned research can fill in those blanks."

I hoped so as well. I hated everything about this. I wasn't sure having the whole picture would help, but I supposed it couldn't hurt. "What time is Shaggy coming by?" I asked.

"I told him I'd text him when I knew when we'd be back."

"I'll text him now," I offered. "We should be at your place by the time he drives out from town."

Shaggy pulled into Tony's drive just as we arrived. Tony went to greet hum, while I went inside to fetch the dogs. All three, including Buddy, trotted over to greet Shaggy with tails wagging. That was a good sign. If Buddy remembered Shaggy from his earlier visit and was happy to see him, I hoped that meant the two would bond, and Buddy would finally have a forever home.

We took the dogs for a walk around the lake. Shaggy tossed a stick as we went, which kept the dogs entertained. His video store was closed on Sundays, but before he committed 100 percent to taking Buddy on a permanent basis, he wanted to see how he did both at his home without the other dogs to act as a buffer, and at the store, where customers came in and out all day. I'd spoken to Brady, who was fine with Shaggy taking him for a trial run, so we worked out the details while we made our way back to Tony's house.

When Shaggy and Buddy had gone, I settled down all the animals and then Tony and I went down to the computer room to look in to Hartford Harrington's past. It was harder to dig up information on someone who had lived before the internet because their lives weren't always available with the click of a keyboard. But Harrington had been a wealthy and influential man, so there was quite a bit of information available.

I sat quietly as Tony's fingers flew over the keyboard. I knew there wasn't anything I could do to help and could probably just as easily have gone upstairs to hang out with the animals, but sitting near Tony while he worked made me feel as if I was helping even if I wasn't, so I sat and waited, fidgeted a bit, then waited some more.

"This is interesting," Tony said.

"What is?" I sat up straighter and glanced at the screen over his shoulder.

"Hartford Harrington was the middle of three children. He was the only one of those three children to survive their teen years."

"His siblings died?"

Tony nodded. "Hartford had an older sister, Estelle. She overdosed on sleeping pills when she was just fifteen. He also had a younger brother, Trenton.

He was killed in a boating accident when he was thirteen."

I furrowed my brow. "It really does sound like the family was cursed. How about Hartford's parents? Did they bail on their children the way he did?"

Tony continued to read, then clicked on a link that led to another. "It looks like Hartford's mother committed suicide when he was ten. So far, I haven't found any evidence that his father didn't raise the children on his own after his wife's death. I'll keep looking."

I leaned forward, placing my hand on Tony's shoulder to get a better look at the screen. "Harrington's mother committed suicide. His older sister took sleeping pills. With the possible exception of Hillary, it appears every one of his children died before reaching adulthood. Hartford seemed to have been of sound mind and body, but it does sound as if the Harrington family might have been dealing with a family curse."

"I doubt there's a family curse, but I think there might be a mental health issue, as we discussed in the truck. Something hereditary," Tony said. He continued to key in search commands. "I haven't been able to find anything about Hartford's grandparents or their parents or siblings, but if I had to guess, a gene was passed from Hartford's mother to his sister. It seems not to have been passed to either male child, which isn't unusual. Most hereditary issues are only passed to a percentage of the children. Based on what Rena Wiggins told us, I'm taking a stab at some sort of schizophrenia, with an onset associated with puberty. I'm not an expert in this subject by any means, so this is just a guess, but it sounded as if Henrietta Harrington suffered from hallucinations accompanied by paranoia."

I frowned. "I still don't understand why Harrington built the house and basically hid his family away from the world. From what we know, it doesn't sound as if either Hudson or Hillary exhibited symptoms, and Henrietta didn't begin to for quite a few years after they moved here, so what would prompt Harrington to do what he did?"

Tony shrugged. "I don't know. There must be a piece to the puzzle we don't have."

"Maybe more than one piece. We still have no idea who the skeleton Jordan Westlake found belongs to."

"True. Call Mike and ask him if he has any news on the identity. It would be interesting to find out how long it was in that closet. At this point we can't determine whether the skeleton was put there while the Harringtons lived there or after all of them were gone."

"I doubt he'll hear anything until at least tomorrow; it's the weekend, and a long-dead skeleton isn't going to be a high priority for the medical examiner's office. I'll make a point to stop by Mike's office while I'm doing my route." I sat back in my chair and stretched my legs out in front of me. "I wonder how much Jordan Westlake knows about the history of the Harrington family and their life in that house."

"I would think he'd have been curious and researched things before moving here. Given the family connection, even if it isn't biological, he might have access to information not available on the internet."

"That's true. I wonder if he'd talk to us."

"It wouldn't hurt to ask him," Tony said. "He was pretty forthcoming when we spoke to him last night."

"I don't have his number, but I can probably get it from Mike." I glanced at the clock. It wasn't that late, but we were at a point where we were stalled with this, and we'd decided to pause on the investigation into my dad. "Maybe I should go home. I left a pile of laundry in my bedroom."

"We haven't had dinner yet."

I shrugged. "I can pick something up or make a sandwich. If we start a game, I'll end up being here late, and I really should get to bed early tonight."

"Okay. If that's what you want to do."

Tony looked disappointed, and I felt bad. We'd never had the chance to just hang out this weekend. "If you want to follow me into town, we can drop off the animals at my place, I can pop a load in the washer, and we can go out for pizza or a burger."

Tony smiled. "That sounds like a plan. Just let me change my clothes."

"I'll pack mine while you do that."

******

By the time we dropped off the animals at my cabin and I'd started a load of laundry, it was after seven o'clock. We decided to head to a local burger joint that featured a good selection of beers and an outdoor deck overlooking the lake. It was crowded, which was to be expected on a Sunday night, but we found a table near the water and settled in with our menus. We were discussing the options when I noticed Jordan Westlake walk onto the deck from the parking area. He appeared to be alone, so I waved to him.

"Are you here alone?" I asked.

"Yes. I don't really know anyone in town yet, but I'm tired of eating alone in that depressing house."

"Join us," I offered. "We haven't ordered yet, so your timing is perfect."

Tony scooted his chair around to make room for the one Jordan pulled over.

"Thank you," he said. "I appreciate the invite. It'll be nice to have someone to talk to other than the ghosts in the house."

"Have you seen any?" I wondered.

"Not yet, but the skeleton in the closet seems to indicate at least one person might very well have unresolved issues in it. To be honest, I thought I knew what I was getting in to, and was even prepared to deal with family ghosts, but the skeleton threw me."

"And you have no idea who it might be?"

"Not a clue."

"I know of six people who died or went missing while living in the house, and it's my understanding all but Hillary were buried in the family plot."

"That's my understanding as well. And there are five headstones. I checked," Jordan assured me. "I guess the only way to know for certain that the bodies that are supposed to be buried in the family plot really are is to dig them up, but I thought I'd wait to see what your brother comes up with before going to that extreme."

"The family history is tragic enough without the added creep factor of a skeleton or dug-up graves," I agreed.

"Do you know much about the family and the house?" Jordan asked.

"Some," I said. "Tony and I have been doing some looking around since you moved in. I never really thought much about the house until recently, but now I'm anxious to know what happened there. Everything we know so far is so sad."

Jordan nodded. "Sad is putting it mildly. Before I inherited the house I wasn't really interested in my family history. Especially not the Harrington side, because I'm not connected by blood. But once I realized there was a huge house on a large piece of property just waiting for someone to show them some love, I was hooked on both."

"We were just discussing the history of the place. One of the questions we had dealt with the reason Hartford Harrington moved his family from San Francisco to White Eagle in the first place."

"As far as I can tell, he made his decision after Hope died."

"Hope?" I asked.

"Hope was Hillary's twin sister," Jordan informed us. "She was killed when she was thirteen, about a year before the family moved to White Eagle."

My hand flew to my mouth. "Oh, no. I'm so sorry. I hadn't heard about a sixth child. How did she die?"

"She ran into traffic and was hit by a bus." Jordan paused and looked around before he continued. "I'm not sure if you're aware of this, but Hartford had two siblings who died when they were young."

I nodded. "We came across some information about his older sister and younger brother."

"The sister killed herself with sleeping pills and the brother died in a boating accident, but there was more to it, I'm afraid. Hartford's grandmother came from a family with its own tragic past. While she seemed fine and lived a long and healthy life, two of her five siblings, both females, committed suicide after exhibiting paranoia that was somehow related to hallucinations they said they'd been having. Hartford's grandmother had three children, two of whom lived full lives, but Hartford's mother, like her mother's sisters, complained of hearing voices in her head and people in their house. She died when Hartford was ten. His sister overdosed a year later after exhibiting similar behavior."

"And his brother? The one who died in the boating accident. Did he suffer from hallucinations as well?"

"No. At least I don't think so, based on what I've found. He drowned when the boat he was sailing in capsized. Hartford was raised by his father. He was aware that the females in the family seemed to have suffered from some mental illness, but he didn't know what it was or feel affected by it. He married and had six children. Hudson, the oldest, didn't exhibit signs of any illness, as expected. He was cautious as Hope and Hillary approached puberty because it seemed to correspond with the onset of the hallucinations. Hillary hadn't yet demonstrated that she'd been experiencing hallucinations, but Hope had begun talking to people who weren't there. She was running from someone only she could see the day she died. Hartford was crushed. According to relatives, he couldn't deal with the possibility that all his daughters would be afflicted with the disease, so he moved the family to White Eagle and, other than supporting them financially, forgot about them."

"That's awful," I gasped.

"It's one of the cruelest and most inhumane things I've ever heard of."

"Did Hillary ever exhibit symptoms associated with the disease?" Tony asked.

"Not as far as I know. I've heard she was fine mentally, although when her father tore her away from her life in San Francisco and moved her to White Eagle, she was about as pissed off as a person could get. I plan to continue my research now that I'm here. From what I could find in family records, diaries, and personal recollections, neither Hillary nor Hudson demonstrated any symptoms of the illness. If he had the gene, Hudson most definitely would have had symptoms by the time he reached his sixteenth birthday."

"Someone told us that Henrietta had hallucinations before she died," Tony said. "I wonder if the younger two did as well."

"Perhaps." Jordan motioned for the waitress to bring a pitcher of beer and three glasses to our table. "When I inherited the house, my first reaction was to sell it. As I said before, I'm not related to the Harrington family biologically, and I have no attachment to the house. I do like to bring old things to new life, though, and I was a bit bored with my life in San Francisco and had been thinking of a change, so I began to consider keeping the place. My older brother reminded me that the house was supposed to be haunted, which only intrigued me more. It was at that point that I decided to look in to the history of the place, and by the time I had most of the facts, I was hooked. My intention when I got to White Eagle was to restore the house and solve the remaining mysteries surrounding the family who lived here."

"It is fascinating," Tony said.

Jordan poured beer into each of the glasses the waitress dropped off. We placed our orders, and then Jordan continued. "In my mind, the only death that seems cut and dried was Hudson's. There aren't any discrepancies regarding who shot him and why. But Hillary's disappearance was never explained, and the deaths of the younger children are shrouded in a certain amount of uncertainty."

"Of course, now you have the added mystery of the skeleton in the closet," I added.

"I understand the two of you enjoy playing amateur sleuth," Jordan said. "I spoke to a man named Hap when I stopped off at his store, and we got to talking about my skeleton. He said you'd most likely come by to talk to me because you enjoyed investigating such things."

"It's true Tony and I do get caught up in whatever mystery is gripping the town. Tony's a genius on the computer and I'm just nosy." I laughed.

"We wouldn't want to do anything you felt was a violation of your privacy," Tony added.

"It's okay," Jordan said. "I'm happy to have some help on this, especially someone familiar with the town and the people who've been around for a while. I'd like us to work together."

"Definitely," I said for both Tony and myself. "Mike will be looking into the skeleton from an official perspective, but he's usually pretty cool about working with us."

"Can the two of you come by the house tomorrow night?" Jordan asked.

We nodded.

"I'll bring a pizza," Tony offered.

"Great. I'll show you around the house, and we can come up with a plan from there."

Chapter 8

Monday, October 22

I started my route the next morning with Hap's store. He would have been a small child when Hillary disappeared but a few years older when Houston was shot. Based on what we'd learned from Rena Wiggins, Houston hadn't gone to school or even left the grounds after the family arrived, but after Hannah died he'd been alone there, with only the nanny and cook. It seemed possible, maybe even probable, that he might have snuck out from time to time. I certainly would have. I couldn't imagine living in that big old house after my entire family had died.

Talk about creepy.

"Morning, Hap," I said as Tilly and I walked in.

"Morning, Tess, Tilly. Did the two of you have a nice weekend?"

"We did. Spent most of it with Tony, who by the way, said the paint I took out to him was exactly the color he was hoping for."

"Glad to hear it. That boy does seem to have some specific ideas. Unlike Mr. Westlake, who knows what he's going to need but can't narrow down the colors at all."

"I heard you spoke to him about paint. It was industrious of you to introduce yourself."

"Introducing myself to a man who seems to be in the market for a whole lot of paint and home remodel supplies is a good idea. I think he's interested in what I have to offer, although, as I said, he hasn't decided on colors yet. Still, I wanted to let him know I was here to see to all his home improvement needs when he's ready."

"Tony and I ran into him at the burger place by the lake last night. He was alone and we'd just arrived, so we invited him to join us. He mentioned meeting you. Seemed like you made an impression."

"Glad to hear it. Did you enjoy your evening?"

"We had a nice time. Jordan knows quite a bit about the Harrington family. We had an interesting conversation."

"I told him you would most likely come snooping around now that there's a skeleton to identify."

"He seemed fine with it," I said defensively. "In fact, Tony and I are seeing him again tonight."

"Great. Feel free to talk up my personalized service. I sure would like to have the chance to provide all his supplies."

"I'll talk you up big if I have the chance. Listen, you were here in White Eagle when the Harringtons were. I don't suppose you remember anything? I know you were just a kid, but it occurred to me that you might have been old enough by the time the youngest boy died to remember him."

"I didn't know him well, but I ran into him from time to time after his sister fell down the stairs and he started sneaking into town. Can't say I blamed him for it. I can't imagine being cooped up in that big old house with so many deaths weighing on me."

"I understand the father didn't want him to leave the house."

Hap shrugged. "Seems like he didn't want any of those kids to leave, but I don't remember him being around to do anything about it."

"What about the nanny? She must have at least attempted to control the situation."

Hap shook his head. "I don't remember there being a nanny. At least not at the end. Guess there might have been one when the mother first died."

I frowned. "Then who took care of the children?"

"I can't say for sure, but it seems the boy might have been looking after himself by the time I started running in to him. He must have had money. I remember seeing him at the diner from time to time. He wasn't real sociable, but that's understandable."

I made a mental note to check into the nanny situation. Rena Wiggins had said she was living in the house up to the point when she was fired, but she didn't know what happened after that. If the nanny quit at some point, you'd think the father would have found someone else. Maybe Hap didn't have the whole story.

"Do you remember anyone the boy hung out with? Maybe another teen living in town?"

"I saw him with Wilbur Woodbine a couple of times."

"The man the older son thought killed his sister?"

Hap nodded. "Wilbur was a simple man and lived close to the Harrington place. I imagine it might have been convenient for the boy to go to Wilbur if he needed something, especially if he believed Wilbur when he said he hadn't hurt his sister. Sure, Wilbur had shot his brother, but from what I understand, that was self-defense."

I scrunched up my nose. "Yeah, I guess. It still seems odd he would befriend a man who was responsible for his brother's death."

"The Harrington place was out there quite a ways, and Wilbur was close by. Beggars can't be choosers, and Wilbur was a nice enough man."

Okay, that was interesting. It was too bad Wilbur wasn't still alive. I'd love to be able to talk to him about what really had happened out there in the woods. "Can you think of anyone else? Someone who's still alive and living in White Eagle?"

"No one comes to mind right off, but I can think on it."

I smiled. "Thanks." I picked up my bag. "Do you think Houston Harrington really jumped to his death as people say he did?"

Hap shook his head. "He had a rough life, but he seemed to be doing okay when I saw him. He had money and seemed fairly intelligent. I heard he even made some noise about trying to find someone who used to work for the family but had been fired. A tutor, I think."

"Rena Wiggins?"

"Sounds right. Maybe he was close to her, but his father hired a nanny who didn't like her, so she was let go."

"Seems like you remember more about Houston than you thought you did."

"Yeah. I guess I must have talked with him a time or two. Heard things from others as well. Been a while, but now that I'm thinking about it, some things are coming back to me. You know who you might talk to is Gordy Rothenberger. He's several years older than me and I think he would have been the same age as the boy. And he lived out there near the Harrington house in those days. In fact, I think he might have lived just down the lane from Wilbur Woodbine. I could see Gordy maybe reaching out to the boy after he lost his whole family."

"Thanks, Hap. I'll stop by his place. If you think of anything else, call me."

"I will, darlin' and don't forget to talk to young Westlake about my services."

"I won't forget."

I decided to use my lunch hour to speak to Gordy. I didn't have his number and wasn't completely certain he still living where he had as a boy, but if he did, his place wasn't all that far off my route, so I wouldn't lose much time checking it out, hoping that was still his home, he was there, and he was willing to talk to me. I wanted to get at least half my route done before then, so I put my head down to avoid eye contact with the people I met along the way. Tilly and I quickened our pace and forged ahead.

******

Not only was Gordy living in the house I remembered, he was home and more than happy to speak with me. Better yet, as Hap had predicted, he'd established something of a friendship with Houston Harrington and had some insight into what might have occurred all those years ago.

"Were you friends with Houston for long?" I asked the man, who sat hunched in a La-Z-Boy recliner.

"Couple of years," Gordy answered. "The woman his dad sent to watch the children was strict; she ruled the house with an iron fist. It got worse after the tutor was fired. Houston used to sneak out at night, and we'd meet up at Wilbur's. He couldn't always get out, so he wouldn't always show up, although I knew he tried. Well, that was until the nanny left and he didn't need to sneak out anymore."

"The nanny left? When?"

"I guess around the time Hannah died. No, actually, I think it might have been before she died. I seem to remember Hannah and Houston were both seen in town from time to time after the nanny left."

"And their father didn't hire a replacement?"

Gordy narrowed his eyes, then shook his head. "No. Now that I've had a moment to think on it, I'm sure once the nanny left it was just Houston and Hannah all alone up there at that big house. Hannah stayed closer to home. I don't know exactly what happened, but at some point she died and Houston was alone."

That didn't sound right. Why would Mr. Harrington leave his children completely alone? Gordy must be mistaken. He was just a teenager himself at the time. He couldn't know everything that was going on in the house.

"Tell me about Houston. What was he like?"

"Smart, even though he'd hadn't been to a real school since he moved to White Eagle. He was a fun guy, even though he had a sadness about him. He didn't have the opportunity to meet people, so other than me and Wilbur, he didn't have any real friends."

"What about after he started coming to town? Did he make friends then?"

"Not really. Not good friends. He'd talk to people sometimes, and I saw him talking to some of the other kids around our age, but it seemed he didn't want to get too close to anyone. He used to visit this one guy sometimes. Owned the bar in town for a long time. Sold it a while back. Heard he died last winter."

"Pike?"

"Yeah, that's right. His name was Pike. I'm not sure how they met, but I remember Houston hanging out in the bar, talking to him. Seems they had something in common, although I'm not sure what."

Pike Porter had lived in White Eagle since the nineteen forties and was murdered last December, so I couldn't talk to him about Houston now.

"Can you think of anyone else Houston might have been friends with?"

Gordy shook his head. "Like I said, he didn't go out of his way to make friends. I think there was a lot of really weird stuff going on at that house, and he didn't want to get himself into any situations where folks would want him to talk about it."

I supposed that was understandable. "Can you remember Houston ever saying he heard voices, or saw people who weren't there?"

"Houston didn't seem sick. I heard about his sister, but Houston was fine. He seemed to have his stuff together better than most people. He even had plans to better his situation. He was going to find the tutor I mentioned before, take his sister, and they were going to leave White Eagle and 'the house of death,' as he called it. He had money. A lot of it. I guess he must have gotten it from his father. He was totally fine, I'm sure of it."

"So why did he jump?"

"Oh, he didn't jump. I don't rightly know what happened, but I do know he didn't jump. Why would he? He'd lived in that house for years. And I'm sure it was hard. But by the time they say he jumped, the nanny was gone, and he was finally free. Nope, Houston didn't jump. If he went out that window, he was pushed. There's no doubt in my mind."

"Do you remember hearing about it when it happened?"

Gordy shrugged. "Sure. There was talk. But that was all it was."

I realized if Houston had been living at the house on his own at the time of his death, there wouldn't have been anyone to report he'd jumped. "Do you remember who found Houston's body?"

Gordy rubbed his chin. I could almost see the gears turning in his head. "You know, I don't rightly recall. I hadn't seen him for a while, so I asked Wilbur about him, and he said Houston was found dead on the patio. It appeared he'd jumped, but Wilbur wasn't buying it either, though we didn't talk about it a whole lot."

So someone found Houston's body and buried it in the family plot, but his two friends didn't have any of the facts. Weird. Unless Houston was killed, and it had been his killer who had seen to the body.

After I left Gordy's place, I went to Mike's office. I still didn't have all the answers, and there was a lot that wasn't lining up, yet the longer Gordy spoke, the stronger was my belief of who the skeleton in the closet belonged to.

"You think the skeleton was the nanny?" Mike asked after I explained my theory.

I nodded. "I spoke to Gordy Rothenberger, who was friends with Houston at the end. He said Houston lived in the house with Hannah after the nanny left. That made me wonder why Houston's father didn't send a replacement. Then I realized it must have been because he didn't know the nanny was gone. No one did, except Houston and Hannah."

"You think they killed her?"

I lifted a shoulder. "I don't know. She could have died of natural causes and the kids hid the body in the closet instead of telling anyone. Gordy said Houston had money. My bet is the father continued to send money to the nanny, which she was supposed to use to take care of the children. Houston must have taken the money and supported himself and his sister until she died. It makes sense. Gordy said he was smart. And that he had plans. He had money and his freedom, which he wasn't likely to risk having taken away by telling anyone the nanny everyone thought was taking care of things was actually dead."

Mike narrowed his gaze. "Your theory actually makes sense. There was definitely something odd going on at that house. Did you know the man who was a stand-in for the local police didn't respond to or verify the deaths of any of the youngest three children?"

"I've heard things that support that, but it seems hard to believe even if the town didn't have a regular police force back then."

"Yet I've been unable to find any documentation that would prove anyone outside the family even knew about the deaths of the youngest children until quite a while after the fact."

I bit my lip. "That means things might not have played out the way everyone seems to think they did. From what I've been told, it sounds as if Henrietta died when she fell down the stairs. At least that was what the tutor, who wasn't at the house at the time, was told by both remaining children and the nanny. The thing is, because there weren't any witnesses, how do we know she fell? She might have been pushed, or maybe falling down the stairs wasn't even how she died. The tutor didn't know Henrietta had died until after she'd been buried."

"You have an interesting point."

"And the tutor was gone by the time Hannah died. It sounds like the nanny might have been gone by then as well. If Hannah and Houston were alone in the house by that point, how do we know Hannah died as the result of an illness? And an even better question, if Houston was alone in the house after Hannah died, which seems to be the opinion of those who knew him, how would anyone know he jumped to his death? How did anyone know he was dead? Who found his body? Was Bennington called in? If not, why not? According to Jordan Westlake, there's a tombstone for Houston Harrington in the family cemetery, but if no one was called in and he was the last remaining family member, who buried him?"

"All very good questions," Mike admitted, "though I'm not sure how we can answer them. It seems like everyone who was involved is dead."

"Yeah." I sighed. "It does seem as if the mystery of the Harrington family might very well go unsolved."

Mike sat back in his chair and drummed his fingers on his desk. I could see he was mulling things over. It was frustrating to have questions it seemed impossible to answer. The only real witnesses to what went on at Harrington House was the Harrington family, and they were all dead. I raised a brow. Or were they?

"What if the Harrington children didn't all die as reported?"

"What do you mean?" Mike asked.

"We know Hillary disappeared and Hudson was shot. Bennington responded to both those calls. But no one seemed to be there for the deaths of any of the younger three children. At least, no one other than the children. What if they didn't die? At least not the two youngest?"

"If they didn't die, where did they go?"

"Gordy said Houston had plans to find the tutor; he'd bonded with her, but she was fired. What if he found her? What if both he and Hannah wanted to escape the prison in which they'd been trapped for years, but they knew their father wouldn't just let them walk away, so they faked their deaths? What if the graves in the little cemetery are empty?"

"I guess there's only one way to know for sure."

Chapter 9

When Tony and I arrived at Jordan's that night, Mike had already spoken to him, and the coffins in the little cemetery had been dug up and examined. As I'd predicted, two of them were empty.

Rena Wiggins had claimed not to have known what had happened to Hannah and Houston, but that didn't mean she hadn't lied. Mike decided to have a chat with her in an official capacity, and during the course of that conversation, she admitted that after the nanny died, Hannah and Houston had stashed her in the closet. Free of the long arm of their father, they'd talked someone into helping them look for her. It took a while because she'd moved away from White

Eagle, but eventually, they were able to track her to her new job in Missoula. From there, they came up with a plan for Hannah and Houston to fake their deaths. They moved in with her, and she told everyone the teens were her niece and nephew. They stayed with her until they were old enough to go out on their own.

Both Hannah and Houston had gone on to live happy and productive lives. Neither had children of their own, which was intentional because of what Hope and Henrietta had gone through, but Hannah had married a man with two young children she'd helped to raise, and Houston had adopted two children with his wife of thirty-five years.

I wondered if Mike would arrest Rena Wiggins when she admitted to her part in the plot. Could she be charged with kidnapping because she'd willfully hidden Hannah and Houston from their father? She was an older woman now, and it seemed as if everything had worked out for the best, so I was relieved when Mike told me he planned to turn a blind eye and leave well enough alone.

Along the way, we managed to find answers for most of our questions. We still didn't know what had happened to Hillary, but we did learn more about Henrietta's death. Hannah told Rena Wiggins the details. Henrietta was having one of her fits, which led to a struggle with the nanny at the top of the stairs. After some hair pulling and face scratching, the nanny had had enough and pushed Henrietta to her death, then made Hannah promise not to tell anyone. She threatened that if she did, she'd be the next sibling to die. Hannah hadn't said a word to anyone until after she'd moved in with Rena.

We also still didn't know the identity of the person who had helped Hannah and Houston find Rena Wiggins. She said that person was still alive, and she didn't want to bring any harm to this kindhearted helping hand. I supposed at this point it no longer mattered. To my mind, whoever had helped the twins had done a good thing and should be allowed to retain their anonymity. Still, I had to admit to being curious. I imagined the Good Samaritan had to be at least eighty, maybe older. There weren't all that many people living in White Eagle now who had been living in town back then and would have been old enough to help with the search. Rena hadn't technically said the Samaritan was still living here, so it wasn't necessary to limit my potential suspects to that pool.

"It looks like you're going to have your hands full with this place," Tony said as Jordan took us to look at the demolition in the kitchen.

"It is a big project. There are four bedrooms and three baths on the third floor, three bedrooms, two bathrooms, and a playroom on the second floor, plus two bedrooms and two baths in addition to the kitchen, living, and dining rooms on the first floor."

"And don't forget the parlor at the front of the house," I added.

"Yes, the parlor," Jordan smiled, "which I plan to turn into a library. The rooms on the first floor seem boxy to me. I have a contractor coming next week to take a look at things. I'd like to take out several walls so the kitchen, dining, and living rooms all flow together in an open floor plan. I'm still not sure what I'm going to do with the bedrooms behind the kitchen. They must have been for household staff. I might open up that space as well and move the dining area. I suppose I'll know better once I have a chance to determine which are load-bearing walls and which can easily be removed."

"It's kind of freaky that everything that was in the house when Hannah and Houston left is still here."

Jordan nodded. "It appears they just up and left. I found clothes in the closets, games set out in the playroom, even dishes in the sink. I'd like to take my time and sort through things. Especially in the bedrooms. And I'd still like to know what happened to Hillary. I spoke to your brother, who didn't seem to think the tutor knew what had happened to her, but somewhere in the back of my mind I have this feeling Hillary must have left a clue behind, waiting to be discovered."

I found I had to agree. It really was too bad we still didn't know what had happened to Hillary. "I do hope you find something, though it's very likely after all this time the questions about Hillary's disappearance will remain unanswered. Especially if she's dead."

"You think she might not be?" Jordan asked.

I shrugged. "Hannah and Houston faked their own deaths to escape the hell in which they were trapped. Hillary disappeared just months after the family moved here, but she was the angriest and most vocal about the situation. She was seen in town on numerous occasions, so she obviously had a means of getting out. Maybe she used the bloody clothes as a decoy and just took off."

"She was just fourteen," Jordan reminded me.

"Maybe she had help. It could even have been Wilbur Woodbine who helped her. He was an adult, so he might have had resources to help her escape, and they did spend time together."

"I guess Hillary running away is something that should be explored. I haven't touched the bedroom I've decided based on the contents was most likely hers yet. Maybe I'll find a clue to where she planned to go if she did take off. Would the two of you like a tour of the place?" Jordan asked. "What's here now won't be for much longer."

"I'd love it," I answered, and Tony agreed.

"Mike said you plan to move the bodies in the family cemetery to the one in town," I commented as we went toward the main living area on the first floor.

"Yes. It seems better that way. None of the people who died while living in this house were happy here. It doesn't seem right to leave them trapped here for all eternity. Besides, I think I'll sleep better without constant reminders of the horror the family endured."

"Moving them does seem like the right thing to do," I said. "This house has such a freaky vibe, but it sounds like once you're finished with it, it's going to be great. Of course, the kids in town will have to find a new Halloween house."

"Halloween house?" Jordan asked.

"That's what they call it. It's really well known, given its violent past and the rumor that it's haunted. It's the sort of place teens dare their friends to run up to and knock on the door on Halloween night."

"I guess I can see that. I hate to spoil everyone's fun, but I think the time has come for a new chapter in this old girl's life."

"You're right. And before I forget, I want to assure you that if you go with local contractors and store owners like Hap, you won't be disappointed."

Jordan grinned. "Did he tell you to say that?"

I nodded. "But it's still true. Hap's a good guy. He's lived here as long as I've been alive and I've never heard anyone say a single negative thing about him."

"Good to know. I'm thinking gray for the walls in this room."

Tony and I paused to look around the parlor.

"Gray walls with white bookshelves would look nice," I said.

"And maybe you can add a gas fireplace on the far wall," Tony suggested. "You'll be glad to have it once winter sets in."

We chatted for over two hours before Tony and I headed back to my place, where the animals were waiting for their dinner.

"What a day." I yawned as Tony drove his truck. "A good day, I suppose, but a long day."

"It did my heart good to know Hannah and Houston didn't die in the house," Tony said, "and went on to live full lives, though the reason the ruse was necessary is heartbreaking. It must be unbearable to be deserted by your own father that way."

I let out a long breath. "It is."

He reached over to grab my hand. "I'm sorry. I wasn't thinking. That was an insensitive thing to say."

I squeezed his hand. "It's okay. I knew you were speaking about Hartford Harrington, not my father, but the not knowing is getting harder and harder. I wish there was a way for us to know why he left. And I know you've warned me that the why might not be pretty, though knowing my dad is a serial killer, or a fugitive, or whatever, still has to be better than wondering."

"I've been working on it, but admittedly not as hard as I could have been. I'll step it up and try looking around on the dark web. Someone has to know something. We just need to find the right someone."

I leaned my head against the headrest and closed my eyes. I let the cool breeze from the partially open window brush over my face. There was something so relaxing about driving at night, when the road is deserted and the horizon is shrouded in darkness. "When I was a little girl, I guess around eight or nine, Dad came home from one of his long-distance gigs with a broken hand and a face that was so beaten and bruised he was barely recognizable. I thought he had been in an accident, but it turned out it was a bar fight. Or at least that's what he told us. I remember Mom was really angry. I'm pretty sure he slept on the sofa right up until he left for his next job. At the time, I didn't understand why my mom was being so mean to him. He was hurt, and I thought she should be taking care of him. It wasn't until after I'd grown up a bit and realized he'd come home with unexplained bumps and bruises a lot more often than could be explained by normal clumsiness that I understood why she was so angry. I suppose he might just have been a drunk who got himself into one brawl after another while he was out on the road, but now I'm wondering if the broken bones, cuts, and bruises weren't the result of something else entirely."

"You think he was doing something other than driving across country when he was away?"

I turned and looked at Tony. "Don't you? Doesn't it seem to you from what we've already found out that he was living a secret life? And now it looks like he's moved on to another secret life. How can I possibly know what's real and what's a cover? I understand there are men who drink too much and get themselves beaten up in the process, but now that I suspect my dad might actually have been doing something we knew nothing about, I'm starting to remember things. Inconsistencies. Unusual actions and reactions. I wish I could talk to my mom about it, but I know I can't. Not yet. If my dad was lying to us the entire time he was with us and she doesn't know about his secret life, I don't want to bring up the possibility until I have facts to back up my suspicions."

Tony turned onto the country road that led to my cabin.

"I think that's a good idea," he said. "As betrayed as you feel, it's going to be even worse for your mom if she finds out her entire marriage was a lie. I know progress has been slow and the clues have been vague enough not to lead us in a solid direction, but I'm committed to working on this as long as it takes."

I smiled. "Thanks, Tony."

"And if you do think of anything, anything at all, even something totally random, let me know. You never know when some seemingly unimportant memory you might have locked in your mind could give us the clue we need to begin to figure this whole thing out."

He pulled into my drive and I sat up taller. I knew the dogs would need to go out, but it was a nice evening despite the storm that was expected to roll in overnight, so I planned to grab a jacket and a flashlight and take them down the trail a short way. The clouds had begun to gather overhead, blocking the light from the moon as they blew past on their way north.

"Looks like that storm is coming," Tony said.

"Yeah. I think it's supposed to be here overnight. I guess we can use the moisture a good rain will provide, but I'm not looking forward to doing my route in it tomorrow."

"At least it isn't supposed to be a cold storm," Tony tried to offer a sliver of comfort.

"True. It's been unseasonably warm, which means the storm will most likely upset the mild temperatures we've been having."

Tony put his arm around my shoulder. "I did hear we might have snow by the end of the week."

"I'm going to take the dogs for a short walk. Do you want to come?"

"Sure."

I fed the cats, got my jacket and flashlight, and we headed out. The wind was just starting to pick up, making the bright yellow leaves that had fallen from the grove of aspens lining the trail blow in a random pattern across our feet as we walked hand in hand, with Titan and Tilly running in front of us.

"Are you busy tomorrow evening?" Tony asked.

"No. Did you have something in mind?"

"We never did string your lights or buy your pumpkins. I thought I'd come by to take care of the lights tomorrow afternoon. Then, when you get off, we can get the pumpkins and maybe grab some dinner."

I leaned my head on Tony's shoulder. "I'd like that. I'll leave the lights on my dining table. Do you still have the key I gave you a while back?"

"I do."

"Okay, then. It seems we have a plan." I paused as the night, silent except for the rustling as the wind filtered through the trees, seemed to wrap itself around us as we journeyed deeper into the forest. "I've missed this. I've missed us," I added. "I'm glad you're done with your project and can take some time off."

Tony turned and looked at me, then put both arms around my waist. "Me too. Even though I've been busy, my life has seemed empty without you in it."

A wisp of hair blew across my face. Tony used a finger to tuck it behind my ear. I could feel my heart pounding as the wind picked up and the bright yellow leaves that had been clinging to the aspens rained down around us. I felt like a response of some sort was required of me, yet I was at a loss for words, so I did the only thing I could think of. I leaned in just a bit and touched Tony's lips ever so lightly with my own. His arms tightened around me as he returned my shy offer. Gentle at first, his lips brushed across mine, creating a tingling that worked its way through my whole body. When I returned his kiss rather than pulling away, as I think he expected me to, his kiss grew firmer. The rain started to fall, but it didn't really bother me. I knew I would always remember this moment in the years to come. Bright yellow leaves and tears from the sky rained down around us, and the world outside our entwined bodies seemed to melt away as I gave my heart to the person who had held it all along.

Chapter 10

Tuesday, October 23

I woke with a smile I couldn't control. Yes, it was pouring rain, and yes, I'd have to spend the day delivering mail in a downpour. And while I was sorry Tony hadn't stayed, I was happy to have some time to myself to relive the memory of those few perfect moments when the world ceased to exist as Tony's lips finally found mine. Not that we hadn't kissed before. We had: a friendly peck of greeting or departure. But in all the years I'd known him, we'd never allowed ourselves to abandon ourselves as we had last night. I wondered what those brief moments in the rain would mean for us. I was both excited and terrified to find out.

Lord, I was a basket of emotions I had no idea what to do with.

Tang saved me from my self-analysis by batting at my face with his paw. He wasn't one to be kept waiting once morning had dawned and breakfast was due. I rolled out of bed, pulled on a heavy sweatshirt, and made my way into the living area of the cabin. I opened the door and let Tilly out, then filled the cat bowls with food and water. When Tang and Tinder were taken care of, I started some coffee, then turned on the television to check the weather, which, unfortunately, predicted more than three inches of rain in the next twenty-four hours. I supposed that meant my Halloween lights would have to wait. I hoped Tony would still come over. Maybe we could just build a fire and share a pizza. It would be nice to snuggle in my cozy little cabin while the storm raged outside. I'd text him later to see what he thought.

I touched my hand to my lips. Again, I wondered where our relationship would go from here. Would things seem strange? Would we begin to feel awkward around each other? Would the most perfect moment of my life turn out to be the one I'd live to regret the most?

Tilly barked, letting me know she was ready to come in. I opened the door, then stood back while she shook about a quart of water out of her thick coat. I grabbed a towel and dried her off, then went into the kitchen to pour myself a cup of coffee. Tilly went over to her bowl and began to wolf down her breakfast. My stomach was too topsy-turvy for food this morning so I'd stick with coffee.

"I think I'm going to leave you home today," I said to Tilly. "No use both of us being miserable. If we get as much rain as predicted, it's going to be pretty awful."

Tilly glanced up at me, then returned her attention to her food.

I looked out the window at the rain coming down in sheets. It was nice and warm inside and I had no desire to head out into the storm. But I had a job to do, so despite my desire to call in sick and go back to bed, I headed to the shower and planned to get an early start on the day.

******

"Morning, Hattie. Something smells good," I greeted Hattie Johnson, Hap's ex-wife and current girlfriend. I think. I'm not 100 percent sure of the legal status of their relationship. They used to be married but had since parted. They lived in separate homes but continued to see each other and, as far as I knew, their relationship was considered to be exclusive.

"Pumpkin-nut muffins just out of the oven," Hattie answered. "Do you want one?"

I glanced out the window at the pouring rain. I was only a quarter of the way through my route, but I was already chilled to the bone. "If it's accompanied by a cup of hot coffee and Bruiser will scoot over and allow me to join him by your fireplace. I'm freezing. It'll be good to warm up for a minute."

Hattie glanced at her rescue dog, who was snoring away the morning. "I think Bruiser will be willing to share, and you look like you need to warm up. That slicker you have on doesn't seem to be doing its job," she observed as I slipped it off and hung it on a coatrack to dry out a bit.

"It's the wind. It blows the slicker up, letting the rain get under it. I love rain if I can sit at home and watch it, but if I have to be out in something, I prefer snow."

"Heard this storm is going to blow though overnight and snow won't be far behind."

Great. I tried to smile as I took a sip of my coffee, but I was already tired and I still had most of my day to go.

"Where is Tilly today?"

"I decided to have mercy on her and let her stay home with the cats. Tony's going to stop by later to let her out. I miss having her with me, but there's no reason for both of us to be miserable."

"Sounds like a decision a good mom would make, and I'm sure Tony doesn't mind helping out. I heard about the mystery you kids have been researching up there at Harrington House. Hap filled me in on Sunday when we had dinner, but he didn't have all the details."

"We've found out quite a bit since I last spoke to Hap." I took a few minutes to bring Hattie up-to-date while I drank my coffee and nibbled on my muffin. "I don't suppose you have any insight about who might have helped Hannah and Houston or what might have happened to Hillary?"

Hattie grew thoughtful. "I have no idea what might have happened to the oldest girl, but I might have an idea who helped the younger two."

"Who?" I asked, forgetting my discomfort.

"You said someone helped them find the tutor right around the time everyone thought they'd died?"

"That's right."

"So that was about sixty years ago?"

"Fifty-nine, to be exact. The tutor said whoever it was is still alive. I figure they'd need to be eighty, or thereabouts. She didn't say for a fact that this person is still in White Eagle, but my gut tells me they could very well be."

"Keep in mind, my family didn't move to White Eagle until after the Harrington House was boarded up and deserted, but something Hap said made me think about Patricia Porter."

"Pike's wife?" I remembered Gordy Rothenberger saying Houston used to hang out with Pike from time to time. And I knew Pike was married to a midwife named Patricia in the fifties.

Hattie nodded. "Hap mentioned that Houston spent time with Pike. He would have been a young man back then. Newly married, from what I understand. From everything I've heard about Patricia, she was the giving and nurturing sort. Just the type to help a couple of kids in need."

"That makes sense, but Patricia's dead."

"One of Patricia's best friends is still alive, and she lived here back then."

Bella, I realized. Bella Bradford hadn't said a thing to indicate Hannah and Houston hadn't died when I'd spoken to her, but then, she wouldn't. Maybe now that we knew the truth, and Mike had said he had no plans to arrest anyone, she'd share the rest of the story.

"I need to talk to her. That will mean I'm never going to finish my route on time, but now that I've come this far, I feel like I need the last few details. Thanks for the coffee and the conversation."

"My pleasure, dear. I hope you find the answers you're looking for."

I decided to finish at least the first half of my route before going over to Bella's. I wanted to find my answers, but I didn't want to be irresponsible. People depended on me to get the mail to them in a timely manner, and that was exactly what I'd do. I'd just need to keep my head down to avoid conversations about the weather. It was the hot topic of the day, but I managed not to be drawn in to chatter about it until I got to Bree's bookstore.

"Did you talk to Mike?" she asked the minute I walked in with her stack of only slightly damp mail.

"I spoke to him yesterday, after he spoke to the tutor."

"Can you imagine keeping a secret like that all these years?" Bree picked up a pile of books and started to shelve them. "I mean, I guess I understand why she did, but wow."

"I'm glad Mike isn't going to pursue the matter. I totally understand why she did what she did and consider her a hero, but some cops might look at it differently."

Bree paused with a book in her hand. "Mike's a good guy. He cares about people. He does his job, but when it comes right down to it, he puts people first. I should have remembered that when I got so mad at him over Donny."

"But if you hadn't gotten mad over Donny, Mike wouldn't have had reason to play your secret admirer and send you gifts at Valentine's Day, and you might not be together today."

"True. I guess things turned out just the way they were supposed to."

"Listen, I have to go so I have time to chat with Bella Bradford during my break. I'll call you later. Maybe we can make plans for the weekend."

"Okay. Try not to catch pneumonia. It's really nasty out there."

Nasty, I decided, was an understatement, but I chose this job and tried to enjoy it in good weather and bad.

By the time my lunch break came around I was exhausted, but I still wanted to talk to Bella. I'd suspected she knew more than she'd let on and remembered she'd been the one who gave me Rena Wiggins's name. I supposed giving us a clue that would lead us to the person who seemed to have most of the answers we were looking for might have been her subtle way of helping us find our answers without betraying a trust. She'd said she didn't know what had happened to Hillary, but she'd never said what she knew about the death of Hannah and Houston. In fact, when we'd asked, she'd steered the conversation to Henrietta's death.

It really did make sense that Bella, along with Pike and Patricia, could have helped those kids. She would have been in her twenties then, so she most likely had resources to help them. Bella, like Rena, had been a teacher, so they might have known each other. And from everything I'd heard about Patricia, she was just the sort to dive in and help out when there was a need. I could see her asking Bella for help.

By the time I arrived at Bella's, I was more than exhausted but determined. She appeared to be surprised to see me when I knocked on her door, but I briefly explained why I was there and she invited me in. I took off my wet outerwear but was still damp beneath it, so I declined the offer to sit on her sofa and instead took a seat on the raised fireplace hearth.

"Thank you for agreeing to talk to me," I started in. "I'm still working on the mystery of the Harrington family and have a few more questions.

First off, let me catch you up with what I've learned since I was here last week."

A thoughtful expression crossed Bella's face as I shared what I knew. When I got to the part about figuring out that Hannah and Houston hadn't really died, she looked surprised but also relieved.

"I've lived with that secret for so long. It was the right thing to do, but still, it was a difficult secret to keep."

"I agree with you," I said, "and Mike thinks so as well. He isn't going to press any charges against Rena or anyone else involved in the cover-up. Based on what I've figured out, it seems as if it might have been Patricia who asked you to help out?"

Bella nodded her head. "Yes, it was Patricia. After the nanny died, Houston started coming into town. He was only fourteen, so I'm not sure why he started hanging out in the bar, but Pike was a nice guy back then, and Houston seemed to enjoy his company, so Pike would give him a cola and they'd chat while he swept up before opening for the day. In the beginning, Pike didn't know the nanny was dead, but eventually Houston told him the truth. He also shared with him his fear of what might happen if his father found out the nanny had passed away, and his desire to track down the tutor who, according to Houston, was the only adult he'd ever really cared about."

Bella took a deep breath and then continued. "Pike talked to Patricia about the situation and they both agreed it would be a tragedy to return the children to their neglectful father. Patricia knew I was a teacher and thought I might know the tutor because of it. As it turned out, I'd met her, but I didn't know where she'd gone after she left here. I agreed to help them track her down. It took a while, but eventually we were successful. Rena wanted very much to help Hannah and Houston, but she was certain their father would never just let them go, so we came up with the idea of faking their deaths. It was easier than I thought it would be. There was already so much speculation about what sorts of things were going on out at the house, no one questioned it when we started a rumor about their deaths. We knew it would be less believable if they disappeared at the same time, so we started with Hannah. She went to stay with Rena Wiggins while Houston stayed behind. He said Hannah had fallen ill and died, that he had buried her, even went so far as to dig up the dirt and provide a headstone in case someone checked, although I don't think anyone ever did."

"No one checked on Houston's story?"

Bella shook her head. "That was one of the saddest parts about the whole thing. I couldn't believe not one person questioned the fact that he buried his sister on his own. It just shows how bad things were back then."

"Wow." I ran my hands through my damp hair. I felt a chill, but I wasn't certain it was from the cold. "Then what happened?"

"Shortly after the rumors surrounding Hannah's death began to slow down, we enlisted Wilbur's help. Houston went to live with Rena, as Hannah already had, and Wilbur started a rumor, which Pike, Patricia, and I supported, that he had gone by the Harrington House to check on the youngest son and found him dead on the patio. It appeared he had jumped to his death from the third-floor window. I was nervous about that one, but no one batted an eye. Wilbur said he'd buried the boy in the family plot and no one looked any further for an explanation. I guess people assumed the nanny moved on after the death of the last child. No one asked about her, but I don't think anyone imagined she'd been dead for quite some time. I know it was wrong of me not to report her death, but my allegiance was to those poor kids."

"And the children's father never came out to check on things?"

Bella tilted her head. "Not as far as I know. I think he left them there to die. Once it was done, he was happy it was over."

That, I decided, had to be the saddest thing of all.

"And Hillary? You said you didn't know what happened to her, but…" I let my thought trail off.

Bella didn't answer right away.

"You do know something," I said.

"I didn't at first. But later, after Houston suggested we bring Wilbur in to help with things, I learned something I hadn't known before."

I paused for a breath, then forged ahead. "Are you willing to tell me what you know?"

Bella looked at me, then down at her hands. She seemed to be struggling with her thoughts, so I waited quietly, hoping she'd trust me enough to share what she'd learned. Eventually, she began to speak. "When Houston first suggested confiding in Wilbur and seeking his help, I was confused. The man had shot and killed his brother, and there was a lot of speculation still that he was responsible for Hillary's disappearance. I said as much to him, and that was when he told me that Hillary wasn't dead, and that he had helped her to escape."

I didn't respond, but I wasn't surprised. In the back of my mind, I had suspected Hillary had done exactly that.

Bella continued. "I guess Hillary and Wilbur had struck up a friendship of sorts. She was miserable being locked up in the house, not allowed to go anywhere, but Wilbur lived close by, so when she did manage to sneak out, it was convenient to go to his place. Like I said before, Wilbur was a simple man with simple needs, but he was a nice man as well, with a lot of compassion. When Hillary asked for his help, he gave it."

"So she ran away?"

"She did. According to Wilbur, she'd been talking about doing it ever since the family had been left by the father. None of the kids were thrilled with the situation, but Hillary was determined not to spend her life subjugated to the will of a madman. She worked out a plan with Wilbur to disappear. I guess she snuck out of the house and left the bloody clothes in the woods. Wilbur drove her to meet a boy she knew in San Francisco who'd agreed to drive all the way out to the Montana state line to pick her up and take her to a cousin of his who lived in New Mexico."

I couldn't help but frown. "I get why she wanted to run away, but I don't understand why she didn't tell her siblings. They went through a lot of worry for nothing."

"I didn't know Hillary, but I agree she sounds like a selfish girl. She wanted what she wanted, and I'm not sure it even occurred to her that she would cause the family all sorts of grief."

"Did she know what happened to Hudson?" I asked. "Did she know he died trying to find out about her?"

Bella shrugged. "I don't know. No one heard from her ever again. I have no idea if she lived a long life or died young."

I shook my head in disbelief. "What a tragedy the whole thing was. Did Wilbur ever tell you what happened with Hudson? Why he was shot? How he died?"

Bella nodded. "Wilbur said Hudson came to his place a couple of weeks after Hillary ran away. He believed Wilbur had killed her and hidden the body, so he showed up with a gun aimed at his chest. Wilbur tried to explain, but Hudson wouldn't listen to anything he said. Everything happened fast. Hudson had the gun and was prepared to fire, so Wilbur grabbed a log from the top of a pile of firewood he'd been stacking and threw it at him. Hudson tried to avoid it, stepped back, and tripped on the trunk of a tree Wilbur had been cutting into pieces. Hudson fell on the gun, which went off when he hit the ground. Wilbur called a friend for help. He went to Pennington, who came out to take a look at things. Wilbur told his story to him, and he decided the physical evidence supported his story. Wilbur was never charged with Hudson's death. The rumor mill tended to bend the truth as it made its way through the community, but I don't think anyone who knew Wilbur thought he'd shoot a man in cold blood. Most were willing to let the story stand."

I thanked Bella, then headed back to town to finish my route. I wanted to fill both Tony and Jordan in on what I'd learned, so I texted them to say I had news, and invited them both to meet me in town at the local pizza place when I'd finished my route. I let out a breath of relief. It seemed we really had been able to wrap up this crazy mystery after all.

Chapter 11

Friday, October 26

The rain had passed, the snow had fallen, and the harvest festival was in full swing despite the weather. Tony and I had arranged to meet Bree and Mike at the haunted house, where we planned to scare ourselves silly before going out to dinner. After that, I planned to go with Tony to his house for the weekend. He'd already stopped by the cabin and picked up my animals and my overnight bag. By some unspoken agreement, we hadn't discussed the kiss we'd shared in the rain since, but I had the feeling putting that particular subject on the back burner had been a temporary action that would be brought to the forefront at some point over the weekend. I found I was both nervous and excited to see what came next.

"Wow, look at the line," Bree, who was dressed in new jeans, a leather jacket, and knee-high boots with a heel much too high for snowy sidewalks, said as we circled around toward the back of the line.

"I guess everyone in town decided to come out on opening night," I agreed. The festival ran the entire weekend and the haunted house would be open through Halloween, but apparently, everyone else in town was as excited to try it out as we were.

"I think there's been a lot of additional hoopla this year because of the change in vendor," Mike offered, mimicking my sentiments exactly.

"The line seems to be going pretty quickly, and we have over an hour until our dinner reservation, so I think we'll be fine," Tony added. "I don't think the walk-through takes all that long once you're inside."

"At least the snow has stopped and the temperature has risen a few degrees," Bree said as she blew into her hands. "Still, I wish I'd brought mittens."

"Here." Mike turned Bree so she was facing him, took her hands in his, and tucked them into the pocket of his jacket, where he warmed them with his own. "Better?"

"Much," Bree answered before leaning forward and kissing Mike on the lips.

I couldn't help but glance at Tony. He winked at me. I knew he was thinking the same thing I was, about our own kiss, but going public with whatever was going on between us wasn't something I was even close to being ready for. He took my hand in his and gave it a squeeze. I returned his offer of affection with a soft smile that felt stiff on my frozen lips.

"I heard Jordan Westlake hired a private investigator to try to find out what happened to Hillary Harrington," Bree said after leaning in close and lowering her voice.

"That sort of surprises me," I said. "It's likely she's dead by now, so I'm not sure what there is to gain by looking for her at this point."

Bree snuggled in closer to Mike. "Jordan has a lot of money, so I don't think the expense is an issue. And I'm sure he's curious. After all, they're family of a sorts."

"I guess that's true. And I do understand the curiosity factor. I was happy to hear she left the area voluntarily, but I have to wonder what sort of person bails on her siblings like that."

"Maybe she was more like her father than the others," Tony suggested.

I guess he had a point. Hartford Harrington seemed to have been a self-centered man who was only concerned about how things affected him. Maybe Hillary *was* more like her father than the others.

"I wonder if Hillary would even want to meet Jordan if he found her and she's still alive," Bree added. "The whole thing might be really weird for her. Jordan is basically the child of the child Hartford adopted to replace his real children when he threw them away. I'm not sure how I would feel about that."

"It's not Jordan's fault," Mike countered.

"Of course not," Bree agreed. "But how would you feel if you found out your dad abandoned you— left you to die, really—then went out and got himself another kid to replace you?"

Sometimes I found myself wondering if that wasn't exactly what happened. Not the leaving-Mike-and-me-to-die part, but after our dad left, had he gone on to have another family? Or had he had one all along, which was what prompted him to fake his death in the first place?

"They're having a cheesy horror movie marathon on television on Halloween night," Tony said, changing the subject. "Do you guys want to come over to my place to watch it? I'll even cook."

"I'm game," Bree said. "I love cheesy movies."

"Me too," I seconded.

"I'd love to come if I don't have to work," Mike answered.

"Can't Frank be on call that night?" Bree asked.

"Sure, if I don't fire him first."

I frowned. "You're thinking of firing Frank?"

Mike sighed. "Probably not, but I'm not happy about the fact that he knew since Jordan arrived in town that Toby was camped out in the woods behind the Harrington place spying on him. What could have been going through his mind to ignore that?"

"I told him that he should tell you," I said without thinking.

Mike raised a brow. I saw his face go slightly red as well. "You knew? Why didn't *you* tell me?"

Good question. "I'm sorry. I should have. I told Frank to talk to you about it, and he said he would. I figured it would be better if it came from him. I guess I should have followed up, but I got busy and forgot about it."

"Luckily for all of us, Jordan wasn't upset about the fact that he had a stalker one of the two law enforcement officials in town knew about and ignored. It was irresponsible of Frank not to run Toby off and misguided of you not to mention it to me."

I looked at Bree with a face I hoped said *help me*.

"Last year they showed *The Blob*," Bree said. I shot her a look of gratitude for diffusing the situation. I knew she hated it when Mike and I argued now that they were an item, so she may have come up with a way to smooth things over even without my silent plea. Mike and I were prone to arguing from time to time, but I could see how it would be awkward for her to be in the middle of it now that we were both so important to her. "The original, not the remake," she continued. "I love those old horror flicks. They're nostalgic, and, being cheesy, not actually too scary."

"My favorite is *The Fog*," Tony said in the spirit of support.

"Remake or original?" Bree asked, seemingly happy to have an ally in her effort to get the conversation back on an even keel.

"Both," Tony answered. "The films are different enough that you can watch both in a single season and not feel like you're watching a rerun. I suppose my favorites are the vampire flicks, though. The really corny ones, like *Count Yorga Vampire*."

"Oh, or *The Creature from the Black Lagoon*," I said, jumping onto the bandwagon.

Thankfully, Mike joined in on the conversation and the tension was forgotten. I hadn't remembered how many awesome classic horror films there were until we started discussing them. I hoped we could find them to stream this weekend as Tony suggested after I expressed an interest in seeing several of my favorites.

"It looks like we're almost to the front of the line," I said as we moved forward. "Are we still good on time?"

Tony looked at his watch. "We should be fine."

"I hope this place lives up to the hype," I said as we inched closer. "After spending time in a real house of horrors this week, I'm afraid it's going to take a lot to scare me."

"Jordan's house is creepy, but things don't jump out at you," Bree said.

"According to Toby, they do," Mike countered with a genuine grin on his face. Leave it to him to find the humor in the situation after all.

******

By the time we'd experienced the scariest haunted house I'd ever visited, then shared a delicious dinner, I was a bundle of nerves. I'd been coaching myself all week and figured I'd be prepared for whatever might happen when Tony and I were alone. Still, now that the time had come, I found myself wanting to flee. This was crazy, I decided. I cared about Tony. I might possibly even love him. He was my best friend first and foremost, and I knew he cared about me. He'd never push for anything I wasn't ready for. I just needed to take a deep breath and remember that.

"Shaggy came by with Buddy today," Tony said, breaking the tension somewhat as we made the drive up the mountain.

"And how are things going?" I asked, happy to have doggy tales to focus on.

"The two seem to be very happy together. Like peas in a pod. Buddy appears to have relaxed, and based on the way he follows Shaggy around, never taking his eyes off him, I'd say a little bit in love. Shaggy is equally happy and dropped off the paperwork for the permanent adoption. He asked me to give it to you."

It was very rewarding to find the perfect placement for a hard-to-place dog.

"I think it's really special the way you care so much about the animals who come through the shelter," Tony said. "I love how you work so hard to place each one in just the right situation. It shows what a huge heart you have. You're a very special woman."

I shrugged. "It's really Brady who makes sure everyone finds the perfect home. I just help out where I can."

"Okay, you're both very special." Tony chuckled.

I smiled but didn't respond. At times like this, when things worked out even better than planned, I did feel special. "The house looks pretty," I said as we pulled onto Tony's private road. "Did you add more lights?"

"A few."

"It looks like more than a few. I bet the astronauts can see your house from space, if there are any up there right now," I added.

"I'm not certain, but I think there are some at the Space Station." Tony pulled up and parked.

I opened my door to slide out onto the snowy drive, hoping my legs weren't shaking so hard as to be obvious. I seriously needed to chill. Deciding to ignore whatever spasms my body chose to have, I focused on the walk ahead of me. As soon as Tony opened the front door, Tilly and Titan came running out to meet us. I bent down to greet them, while Tony grabbed an armload of firewood from the pile stacked near the front door and carried it inside. The dogs would need a bathroom break, so I left the door open a crack so they could get back in rather than calling them inside with us now. Tang and Tinder were both curled up on Tony's sofa. They looked up when we entered the room but didn't bother to get up.

"There's a bottle of wine on the counter if you want to pour us glasses while I start the fire," Tony informed me.

Wine sounded good. Something to calm my nerves was exactly what I needed. I called out my assent, then headed to the kitchen while Tony began balling up newspaper and stacking logs. I turned on the light and looked around the room. It appeared as if Tony had finished hanging his wall art since I'd been here last. The dark tones and natural materials provided for a sharp contrast that was really magnificent. There were soft touches as well, such as the window seat, to bring everything together. It really was the most awesome kitchen I'd ever seen.

After pouring two large glasses of wine, I headed back into the living room. Tilly and Titan had come back in and were sitting next to Tony as he worked on the fire. When he saw me enter the room, he stood up and turned to me. My heart started to beat erratically as I took in the thick brown hair that brushed his collar, his expressive brown eyes that seemed to shine with affection, and the curve of his generous lips, which I'd been fantasizing about all week. I handed him a glass and took a sip of my own.

"I see you finished the kitchen," I said conversationally.

"I did. Initially, I couldn't decide whether to rehang the old art or buy something new. I liked the art I had, so I just rearranged it a bit."

"I like it. It looks nice."

Tony must have noticed my hand was trembling because he set down his glass, then took mine and set it next to his. He put his hands on my waist and pulled me close. I thought he was going to kiss me, but he hesitated, then ran a finger down the side of my cheek and looked deep into my eyes. "Don't be nervous, Tess. It's just me. It's just us. Nothing is going to happen you don't want to happen."

I gulped a huge breath of air. "I know. I don't know why I'm nervous. It's silly."

"It's not silly." Tony leaned forward just a bit and kissed me very lightly on the lips. He pulled back just a bit. "Okay?"

I nodded.

He kissed me again. This time, slightly harder and slightly longer. If my legs weren't shaking before, they certainly were now. I wound my arms around Tony's neck, partly to pull him closer and partly to have something to hang on to.

"Do you want me to stop?" Tony whispered against my neck.

"No."

Tony tightened his arms and deepened the kiss once again. I felt my body lean into his as he accepted my weight. His lips were hard and soft at the same time. I could feel his heart beating under my hands, which I'd rested on his chest. The room began to fade away as I gave in to the sensations I was feeling, and I actually let out a little cry of protest as he leaned back just a bit.

I looked into his eyes. He looked back into mine. I wanted to demand that he not stop, but something told me to wait.

After taking a few breaths, he spoke. Softly. Meaningfully. Honestly. "I love you, Tess. I think I've loved you since the first moment I met you in middle school. I've been waiting a long time for this, but I can wait longer. If you aren't ready to go where this seems to be taking us, I can wait."

I put my hands on Tony's face and pulled it toward mine. "I'm ready," I whispered against his lips in the instant before they devoured me.

Chapter 12

Saturday, October 27

I struggled to find my way out of the deep sleep I'd fallen into. I'd been so content, and it had been so peaceful, but something was beeping, pulling me toward wakefulness. I opened my eyes slowly and glanced at the clock on the bedside table. It was seven minutes after three o'clock in the morning. I glanced at the window, which overlooked the lake, to see that the snow had started up again. It took me a minute to remember why I was in Tony's bed; then I felt the weight of his arm lying across my waist and the warmth of his large, fit body behind me.

"Tony," I said as I struggled to get my bearings. I turned slightly and brushed his lips with mine. "Wake up. There's a noise coming from your phone. A god-awful noise for this time of the morning."

Tony stirred just a bit but didn't wake up. I nudged him one more time, a bit more forcefully. The guy was certainly a sound sleeper.

"Tess?" he asked when I shoved his arm away from my body.

"Your phone. There's an alarm or something."

Tony swore, then rolled over. He picked up the phone and silenced the obnoxious noise. I let out a sigh of gratitude that silence had returned to the room.

"Did you set your alarm?" I asked as I rubbed the sleep from my eyes. "Do you have something to do or somewhere to be?"

The dogs were awake now and thumping their tails on the floor while resting their faces on the mattress. I leaned over to pet Tilly.

"It's not that kind of an alarm," Tony said as he groaned and sat up. "It's synched with one of the computer programs I'm running. It alerts me when it gets a hit."

I sat up as well, pulling the sheet across my breasts. "A program? Which one?"

"My facial recognition program."

"My dad," I said, knowing it was true. "You have a hit on my dad."

Tony nodded. "It can wait."

I stood up and began pulling on my clothes. "No," I said with a lot more conviction than I felt, given the fact that I'd woken in Tony's arms for the very first time and was now walking around the room looking for my underwear. "It can't wait."

Tony stood up, crossed the room, and pulled on a pair of jeans and a sweatshirt. He padded across the floor in bare feet and let the dogs out through the bedroom slider. I pulled on a heavy sweatshirt and a pair of socks, then headed to the kitchen to make coffee. Tony went downstairs while I waited for the coffee to perk and the dogs to return.

"Dang it, Dad," I said into the empty room. "Your timing could have been better." I realized as I poured the coffee into mugs that I would never again have the opportunity to wake slowly in Tony's arms after making love with him for the very first time. The knowledge made me feel sad, but I didn't suppose that *first* didn't hold all that much importance as long as there were seconds, thirds, and fourths. Once I'd decided to relax, the evening had been magical. I don't know why I'd been so scared when what we'd had together had felt so perfect I knew it had to be right.

The dogs were back by the time I'd poured the coffee, so I crossed the room to let them in. It was snowing fairly hard and their coats were covered with the white stuff. I found a towel and dried them off, then fed all the animals and went downstairs.

"So, what do we have?" I asked as I handed Tony his coffee.

He set it down, then pulled me into his lap. He drew me in for a deep kiss before answering.

I couldn't help but smile. "That was nice." I rested my hand on Tony's face. "But it could have waited until after you filled me in."

"Actually," Tony said as he kissed me one more time, "it couldn't."

Yeah, I thought. It really couldn't.

Tony turned his attention back to the screen, so I slid off his lap and sat down in the chair next to him. "We have a hit?" I asked. "Did your program find another photo of my dad?"

"It did," Tony answered.

"Where?"

"Eastern Europe. You can't tell by the background where the photo was taken, but if you match up the date and time stamp with the time we received the hit, the photo would have been taken in Eastern Europe."

I felt my heart stop beating. "The photo came to us in real time? We have a photo of my dad that was taken today?"

"Unless we're being fed a decoy, which we should keep in mind is possible, it appears the photo was taken right about the time we got the hit."

"So we know where my dad is."

"Was." Tony turned the screen so I could see it as well. "Not only is Eastern Europe a large area, but, based on what I can make out in the photo, it appears as if your father was boarding a private jet. My guess is, wherever he was when the photo was taken, he's long gone now."

"To where?"

Tony ran his hands over his face. I could sense his frustration. "I don't know. I can't make out anything on the plane that would help me track the ownership or location of the plane, and I can't see enough in the background to even know where the plane was taking off from. The only thing we seem to have is when."

"Do you think the time and date stamp are accurate?"

Tony frowned. "Given everything we've found since we've been searching for your father, the one consistent theme is illusion. Nothing has really been as it seems. I have no reason to believe anyone would intentionally provide us with a false lead, but it does seem as if your father is connected to someone in high places. So maybe."

"What now?" I asked.

Tony took my hand. "I don't think it will do us any good to run off to Europe, although I would very much like to experience it with you sometime. I have a friend who might be able help me track down the location where the photo was taken. I'll call him and ask him what he can find out."

"So we have nothing." I groaned.

"Not nothing. Unless we find out the stamps have been tampered with, we now know your father is still alive. The most recent photo before this one was taken two years ago."

"True."

"And we know he has the ability to travel internationally. That requires identification, which tells us that whatever fake papers he's using, it has deep roots, which means it was created by a pro."

"I'm not sure if that makes me feel better or worse." I ran my hands though my hair.

"I know. I'm afraid your search for answers is bound to be a marathon, but each new clue tells us something we didn't know before. Give me a minute to make a few calls, then I'll make you some breakfast."

"Okay." I stood up. "And thanks."

Tony stood up and pulled me into his arms. "I wish I could make this easier for you. I hate seeing you struggle like this."

"You are making it easier. You make everything easier for me. You warned me this would be hard, and I want you to know I can take whatever ends up being thrown in our direction."

"I know. You're the strongest woman I've ever met. But it does concern me that we seem to be being fed information. First the photo of your mom on the bridge just showed up in my email. I'm not running a facial recognition program on her, so what's with the email? Who sent it and why?"

I frowned. "Good question."

"And then the photo this morning. It seems a bit too calculated to be trusted completely. I'm not saying it isn't legit, but something about it feels off." Tony ran a finger down the side of my face. "I want to find your answers, but I don't want you to get hurt. I don't know what I'd do if anything happened to you."

I placed my hand on Tony's cheek. "I know you're scared for me, and I'm scared for you. I didn't say it last night, but I want you to know I love you too."

USA Today bestselling author, Kathi Daley, lives in beautiful Lake Tahoe with her husband, children, and grandchildren. When she isn't writing, she likes to spend time hiking the miles of desolate trails surrounding her home. Kathi enjoys traveling to the locations she writes about to generate inspiration and add authenticity to her descriptions. Find out more about her books at www.kathidaley.com